INTO *the* HEART *of* MIDDLE-EARTH

A Spiritual Journey for the Hobbit at Heart

INTO the HEART of MIDDLE-EARTH

Exploring Faith and Fellowship in J. R. R. Tolkien's *The Lord of the Rings*

KAITLYN FACISTA

Founded in 1865, Ave Maria Press is a ministry of the United States Province of Holy Cross.

www.avemariapress.com

Paperback: ISBN-13 978-1-64680-365-1

E-book: ISBN-13 978-1-64680-366-8

Cover images © Getty and Unsplash.

Cover and text design by Andy Wagoner.

Interior illustrations by Kaitlyn Facista.

Printed and bound in the United States of America.

Library of Congress Cataloging-in-Publication Data is available.

To those
who seek light
and high beauty.

CONTENTS

Preface

A Spiritual Journey

If my life is a tapestry of thought and memory, Middle-earth is a thread of gold woven in amidst the deepest hues. It is a thread I didn't notice for a long time, laced into a quiet and steady pattern, but as I turn to look back on the years of my life I can suddenly see it clearly. At times, the world of *The Lord of the Rings* has been a spark igniting my own wonder and creativity; other times, it was an anchor holding me fast to my own reality. In the darkest nights, it was a guiding star, illuminating the world and kindling hope amidst doubt.

My earliest memories of Middle-earth are of watching the film adaptations directed by Peter Jackson, a trilogy of cinematic brilliance that set the tone for my teenage years. More than twenty years after the release of the first installment, this experience of seeing the films before reading the books has become increasingly common. Like many new fans, I was prompted by these films to pick up the books they were based on and soon found myself immersed within them. In those days, it became a home away from home; it was a means of grounding myself in an imagined world that somehow felt real.

Stepping into Tolkien's world for the first time was life-changing. Suddenly I felt the cool breeze upon the hillsides of the Shire. I found respite in the woods of Lothlórien. I stumbled up the slopes of Mount Doom with Frodo and Sam into the heart of Mordor. I claimed the One Ring as my own. Along with it, I fell into the fire and I was surprised to wake up and discover I had made it out alive. I was pierced with a "joy like swords" on the Field of Cormallen, washed over with the dawning of a new age. I caught glimpses of myself in every character, and I learned more about myself and my own world with the turn of every page. I had entered into Middle-earth and would not return home unchanged.

Every so often I am reminded that I am really, really, exceptionally into *The Lord of the Rings*. I picked up the books at age eleven and suddenly more than twenty years have passed but I haven't put them down. Middle-earth seems to sneak its way into every corner of my life until one day I'll catch my reflection in the mirror and realize I'm wearing *Lord of the Rings* socks, a *Lord of the Rings* sweater, carrying my baby in a *Lord of the Rings*–themed baby carrier, and drinking tea out of a *Lord of the Rings* mug. On the wall behind me is a bookshelf full of *Lord of the Rings* books and artwork, and on my computer are thousands upon thousands of words typed in discussion of *The Lord of the Rings*. I've fallen headfirst into other stories and fandoms throughout my life, but nothing has ever had such a lasting impact as Middle-earth. This fictional world has changed the way I see and approach my own world; it's as if I now see through Middle-earth-tinted glasses. The green leaves on the trees seem brighter than before, and the realization strikes me that I am more connected to the real world than I had ever imagined.

Middle-earth does not exist outside of words on a page, and yet it sometimes feels more real than the ground beneath my feet. Within Tolkien's books, I've encountered stories that pierce my heart and seem to gain new meanings with every re-read. The world he built is deep and vast and overwhelming to the point where it feels indescribable at times. I find myself returning to Middle-earth so frequently that I've begun to wish I could take a piece of this world home with me. This is a perilous and often disappointing desire because the beauty of myth and story-telling can be lost along the journey home.

It's difficult to fully communicate the wonder of Middle-earth to someone who has never been there. Tolkien explained this feeling in his essay "On Fairy-Stories," writing, "The fairy gold too often turns to withered leaves when it is brought away. All I can ask is that you, knowing these things, will receive my withered leaves, as a token that my hand at least once held a little of the gold." These pages are my withered leaves. I hope this book, however tarnished or frail compared to Tolkien's own masterpiece, will inspire you to venture into Middle-earth to find gold of your own.

Finding My Spiritual Home

Before I became Catholic, I felt adrift, untethered, lost. I had given up on the thought of belonging to any church or religious community. I felt as if I was stumbling along a trail in the dark trying to find my way home. Encountering Catholicism was like turning on the lights.

I have always believed in God but never felt like I was at peace in other Christian communities. My late early twenties were a time of searching for somewhere I could belong. Looking back on it, I feel confident that this journey was guided by Providence, a small star twinkling above the cloud-wrack of my own doubt and restlessness, leading me to a place I could feel spiritually at home. It began by sifting through a list of Christian denominations, learning what I could about each one. After a dozen visits to different churches and a few months of considering Lutheranism, I felt called to look into Catholicism.

Along the way I somehow discovered that J. R. R. Tolkien had been a devout Catholic. I joked with my husband, "If it's good enough for Tolkien, then it's good enough for me." But in the back of my mind, the thought lingered. In truth, this seemingly random moment marked the beginning of my own journey toward the Catholic Church. After years of wandering in Tolkien's works, I now began to cautiously step into a study of Tolkien's life and the faith that nourished him.

I didn't want to drift from church to church anymore; I wanted something permanent. Together, my husband and I began to learn as much as we could about the history, teachings, and lived faith of the Christian Church. I learned that the tradition of the Catholic Church could be traced all the way back to the first Christians.

Through reading the letters of St. Ignatius of Antioch and other church fathers I also came to believe in the Real Presence of Christ in the Blessed Sacrament; this was not taught by any of the other denominations I'd encountered. If I believed Jesus was God—and I did—I wanted to belong to the church that most closely resembled the one Jesus founded. If Christianity is a tree made of many branching denominations, I wanted to cling to its roots. Ultimately, I came to believe that the Catholic Church was where I would belong: a hallowed body made up of imperfect people, rooted in the history and tradition of Christianity and guided by the Holy Spirit toward goodness.

Years after my conversion, I was surprised to come across one of Tolkien's letters that summed up my own beliefs so well. Tolkien writes,

> I myself am convinced by the Petrine claims, nor looking around the world does there seem much doubt which (if Christianity is true) is the true Church, the temple of the Spirit dying but living, corrupt but holy, self-reforming and rearising. But for me that Church of which the pope is the acknowledged head on earth has as chief claim that it is the one that has (and still does) ever defended the Blessed Sacrament, and given it most honour, and put it (as Christ plainly intended) in the prime place. (*Letters*, 250)

In the winter of 2013, my husband's medical schooling had brought us to England for training. There, I attended daily Mass with our infant daughter and was joined by my husband on his days off. Our frequent attendance was noticed by the parish priest, Fr. Tom, who took an earnest interest in our formation. Fr. Tom agreed to meet with us several times and, after obtaining permission from his bishop, he shared that we would be able to enter into the Church the very next month. In January 2014, my husband, our daughter, and I were received into the Catholic Church. We were thousands of miles away from home and yet had now finally found our spiritual home. The ceremony was quiet and lonely, but the nave was filled with poinsettias and the light shone through the stained glass across the humble stone church. I felt a profound peace in the stillness and simplicity of it all.

The following day, we took a train to Oxford where we made our first pilgrimage as new Catholics. We attended Mass in Oxford, where we were able to receive the Blessed Sacrament as part of the congregation for the first time. We visited the Oxford Botanic Garden, where I sat under the same black pine tree that Tolkien had spent countless hours beneath; we had lunch at The Eagle and Child, a well-known spot for Tolkien tourism, as it was one of the favorite meeting places of the Inklings. Tolkien's works had always been a source of comfort and joy to me, but now his life had become the catalyst for finding my own spiritual home, and I am so grateful. It felt fitting that my first pilgrimage would be a Tolkienian one.

A few weeks later, our family returned to the United States and life carried on. We continued to move frequently as my husband continued his medical training, and our family grew as we welcomed new children along the way. I've since had the opportunity to return to Oxford multiple times, and each time I'm filled with a sense of wonder and gratitude for the life of Tolkien and his works.

Finding and Forming Community

Being a Tolkien fan can sometimes be a lonely experience, as *The Lord of the Rings* continues to remain a relatively niche narrative when compared to other fantasy worlds. Most people have at least heard of Middle-earth but couldn't tell their Sauron from their Saruman. Despite the success of Tolkien's works worldwide, discussions of the Fall of Gondolin don't exactly light up the crowd at dinner parties; and elves as important as Fëanor and Celebrimbor are unfortunately not household names. (They should be.) Something as immersive and brilliant as Middle-earth naturally produces the desire to share about it with others, but sometimes that's easier said than done.

As a new stay-at-home mom to my own little hobbits, I discovered that opportunities to connect with other Tolkien fans were few and far between. So, as any good millennial would do, I turned to the internet in hopes of connecting with other folks who might be as fascinated with the minutiae of Middle-earth as I was. And as a new Catholic who was inspired not only by Tolkien's works but by his faith as well, I was also eager to find a community with which to dive into the religious themes woven into his stories. I soon found that the spaces I was searching for didn't really exist at the time (or if they did, I couldn't find them). So I created one: In 2017, I founded the Tea with Tolkien community. With an emphasis on nurturing fellowship as inspired by Tolkien's example, I set out to build an online space in which Tolkien fans could connect with each other in a unique and authentic way.

Tea with Tolkien is a free online community inspired by the life, works, and—specifically—the Catholic faith of J. R. R. Tolkien; unlike many other Tolkien-focused communities, discussion of Tolkien's religious influence is encouraged alongside that of his love of language, mythology, and history. All are welcome within our community regardless of belief, but we place an emphasis on respectful dialogue when it comes to discussions of religion and faith.

Our community is "fundamentally Catholic" in the same way that *The Lord of the Rings* is fundamentally Catholic—it is foundational to our community but not intended for a purely Catholic audience and very deliberately not meant to be an online crusade. Our community's primary focus is a book club that explores the works of Tolkien and encourages meaningful discussions. Along the way, we have also grown into a tight-knit community that shares our lives together online. You can learn more at www.teawithtolkien.com.

It's now been almost ten years since our community first began, and I have had the privilege of meeting and becoming friends with so many passionate, creative, insightful, and kindhearted people because of it. I've been strengthened and challenged in my beliefs, had my eyes opened to new interpretations, and been inspired by so many fans who approach Tolkien from different perspectives and experiences than I do. I've grown in my own understanding of Tolkien, my faith, and the world around me because of this community.

I am so grateful for the opportunity to share this book with you. Whether you're a long-time member of the Tea with Tolkien community or you're discovering us through this book, I hope you feel at home here. Regardless of your religious background or personal beliefs, I hope the perspective from which I write might shine a new light on the life and works of J. R. R. Tolkien and prompt you to reflect on what Middle-earth means to you.

Being a Hobbit at Heart

In the earlier stages of drafting this book I would often doubt myself, wondering if I was the right person to write it. I'm not the perfect homemaker, nor do I have the perfect hobbit aesthetic. I don't bake sourdough bread. I don't have any chickens. I'm not particularly outdoorsy or skilled in the garden. I don't even dress in bright colors. I drink too much iced coffee and paint my fingernails black while listening to emo music. I'm hardly a hobbit at heart, *I used to think*. But I have come to learn over the time I've spent writing this book that being a hobbit at heart is so much more than outward appearances. It is about grounding yourself in goodness, finding your courage, and fixing your gaze on the star of hope that guides you. It doesn't matter if you hate mushrooms, or accidentally kill all of your houseplants, or prefer minimalism to the quaint clutter of Hobbiton. Together, however imperfectly, we can follow in Frodo's footsteps.

I have also questioned what I'm doing writing a book about hobbits while the world is burning. Surely there are more pressing topics at hand, surely I could be doing *more*. I wonder if Tolkien ever felt this way, too. War, injustice, oppression, and suffering ravage the earth, never resting. Sometimes it feels all-consuming, suffocating. But it is in these times that we can look to Tolkien's works for the reminder that "evil labours with vast power and perpetual success—in vain, preparing always only the soil for unexpected good to sprout in" (*Letters*, 46). Evil cannot conquer forever! In the end, it was not the might of men or elves that unmade the power of the Ring: It was the hobbits, in their unassuming frailty, who brought about the downfall of Sauron. Though you may feel small, remember Frodo and take heart; never resign yourself to despair.

A Note on Citations

Throughout the text of this book, I have made parenthetical references to Tolkien's writings so that interested readers may further explore his writing on their own. Here is an explanation of how these citations will appear:

Letters: Excerpts from *The Letters of J. R. R. Tolkien: Revised and Expanded Edition*, edited by Humphrey Carpenter, have been abbreviated to *Letters*. The numbers listed reflect the number assigned to each letter by the editor.

The Lord of the Rings has been abbreviated to *LOTR*. Excerpts from *The Lord of the Rings* will be cited by book and chapter, keeping in mind that *The Lord of the Rings* consists of six volumes (*The Fellowship of the Ring* comprises Books I and II, *The Two Towers* comprises Books III and IV, and *The Return of the King* comprises Books V and VI).

The Silmarillion has been abbreviated to *Silm*.

Unfinished Tales has been abbreviated to *UT*.

Names: Several of Tolkien's characters and locations have more than one name. When applicable, I have opted for the most commonly used name. For example, Melkor will be referred to as Morgoth, his later-given name. For the sake of simplicity, Aragorn II and Denethor II will be respectively referred to as Aragorn and Denethor.

Introduction

Welcome to Middle-earth

Elen síla lúmenn' omentielvo. A star shines on the hour of our meeting.

Welcome to Middle-earth. Here, mythical monsters roam across a detailed map, ordinary people become heroes in their own right, and the great tales of the world unfold before your eyes. Here, we encounter a world filled with heroism and fellowship that shines light against darkness. These themes are timeless and versatile, affording themselves an applicability that transcends cultural divides. And yet by experiencing them in a world unlike our own, they become amplified and heightened by the element of fantasy, inspiring both wonder and a sense of realism.

Because Tolkien's life was so rich with experience, from joy to tragedy and everything in between, his stories speak to each of us differently. We might never fight dragons or orcs, but we will face moments of our own that similarly require courage, fortitude, and action. We will never need to resist the designs of Sauron, but we will have to overcome temptations of our own. We will never be tasked with carrying the One Ring to its destruction, and yet the weight of our own burdens might feel just as overwhelming. Tolkien offers us a world full of both light and darkness, a world with sorrow as deep as an ocean and joy as radiant as the sun.

More than anything, Tolkien offers us a choice. If you long to step outside of yourself, Tolkien offers a new path to tread. If you've found yourself searching for a sense of identity or purpose, Tolkien offers a perspective with which to see yourself in the grand scheme of history. If you feel small, unimportant, unloved, lost, or unworthy, Tolkien offers characters in whom you can see yourself more clearly; he reminds us that it is often the small and seemingly unimportant folk who make the biggest differences. If you struggle to make sense of our primary world, Tolkien offers a way to understand it by shining a light on his "secondary world." If you feel desperate or lonely, Tolkien offers a common ground through which you might connect with others and form genuine community. Through his own experiences of war, death, grief, new life, fellowship, ritual, and prayer, Tolkien was shaped as a man and writer, and in turn, his stories can help to shape us if we let them.

There are so many different facets to Tolkien fandom and scholarship, and each individual reader may approach Tolkien's works in a different way. Each of us may find one aspect of this world more interesting than another or may be more well versed in one corner of this world than another. (If you come across any unfamiliar characters or stories, don't worry; you'll find an overview of Tolkien's story and framework in appendix A.) This diversity has resulted in a bright and bustling public square of interpretations, theories, takeaways, and beliefs surrounding Tolkien's works and is a part of what makes our community such a beautiful place.

Because of my background, upbringing, and experiences, I have found myself very interested in and inspired by the role Tolkien's Catholic faith played within his life and the creation of his literary works. This is my particular area of expertise and the perspective from which this book is written. I am also passionate about reminding readers that mine is not the only valid perspective. To put it simply, Tolkien is for everyone. In a world that encourages division and separation, Tolkien's works can serve as a bridge to bring people together. This book is a reflection of the heart and mind of one Tolkien fan shared with another and does not seek to dominate or discourage other hearts and minds. Instead, it is my hope that this book will kindle a fire in your heart, illuminating your own path without dictating it.

Tolkien does not tell us how to live, but he shows us how it is possible to live well. In *The Lord of the Rings,* he presents heroes we can admire and emulate as well as tragedies that can serve as cautionary tales. By embarking on these adventures alongside our beloved characters, we too can return home somehow changed. To soften our hearts and open ourselves up to the potential for change is scary work, but in the end I believe it is worth it. So when we read Tolkien, it can be like looking into Galadriel's Mirror: Here, we will encounter "things that were, things that are, and things that yet may be" (*LOTR*, Book II, ch. 7).

Peering into the Mirror of Galadriel was perilous and yet also fortuitous. Galadriel offered the chance to both Frodo and Sam in Lothlórien, explaining that in looking they might "learn something, and whether what you see be fair or evil, that may be profitable, and yet it may not. Seeing is both good and perilous" (*LOTR*, Book II, ch. 7). After gazing into the mirror, Frodo and Sam both began to understand the weight of their tasks more tangibly. The mirror showed them what was at stake, a vision of things that might come to pass. In seeing and learning, they walked away with strengthened resolve and a firm commitment to their tasks.

This book will ask you to look at your own faith and convictions, examine what you value and what you hold dear, and take steps toward cultivating the life you were meant to live. In this book, you will be introduced to many of the core themes and concepts of Tolkien's mythology. Hobbits are the through line for both *The Hobbit* and *The Lord of the Rings* and represent the everyman, so we will focus on them primarily. But if you're more of a dwarf at heart, or an elf, that works too.

Together we will begin a journey of nourishing the body, mind, and spirit as inspired by different characters, locations, and themes seen in *The Lord of the Rings*. We will work both to identify our core values and to craft a life that supports these values, with Tolkien's heroes as our inspiration.

Who Was J. R. R. Tolkien?

John Ronald Reuel Tolkien was a philologist, professor of Anglo-Saxon language and literature, and author most popularly known for his stories of hobbits, elves, and magic rings set within his invented world of Middle-earth. Born in 1892, Tolkien would be shaped in his early years by the death of his father in 1896 and the death of his mother in 1904. While his time with his father had been brief, Tolkien's mother, Mabel, had devoted considerable time and effort to the education of John Ronald and his younger brother, Hilary, instilling in them a sense of wonder along with intellectualism.

In 1900, Mabel had converted to Roman Catholicism, and her two sons followed shortly after. Their conversion was met with staunch disapproval by her Protestant family, who withdrew their financial and emotional support in response. Mabel worked tirelessly to provide for her sons, yet the small family struggled materially. Despite these hardships, Mabel and her sons found a spiritual home at the Oratory of St. Philip Neri in Birmingham, where the family's new faith was nourished and strengthened. Tragically, Mabel grew ill and was diagnosed with diabetes in 1904, passing away only a few months later. The Tolkien boys now found themselves orphaned.

Tolkien later noted a correlation between his mother's early death and her family's objection to her conversion, seeing her as "a martyr indeed" who had sacrificed her own health to "ensure us keeping the faith" (*Letters*, 142). After their mother's passing, the Tolkien boys were left in the care of an aunt but for all intents and purposes were raised by an oratory priest and friend of the family, Fr. Francis Morgan, a man Tolkien would later call his "second father" (*Letters*, 332). It was during these years, under the guidance of Fr. Francis, that Tolkien developed a deep passion for and understanding of his Catholic faith, which would remain with him for his entire life. At the same time, he continued to grow into a remarkable linguist and lover of literature, becoming proficient in Latin and Greek as well as beginning to invent languages of his own. Tolkien's formative years at King Edward's School in Birmingham were buoyed by a tight-knit friend group who called themselves the TCBS, short for the Tea Club and Barrovian Society.

The end of Tolkien's childhood largely coincided with the outbreak of the First World War. Tolkien enlisted in the British Armed Forces in 1915, shortly after completing his undergraduate degree; he and Edith Bratt were married just before he was posted to France. After training, the war brought him to the Somme, the scene of one of the bloodiest battles of modern history. Tolkien contracted trench fever, for which he was ultimately discharged and returned to England by the end of 1916.

In 1925, Tolkien accepted a position as a professor of Anglo-Saxon language and literature at Oxford, where he would spend the bulk of his professional career. Though he had composed bits and pieces of his own mythology throughout his youth, it was at Oxford that Tolkien's vision for Middle-earth finally began to take shape. He wrote the first line of *The Hobbit* when a sudden inspiration struck while grading essay-books, and the tales of Middle-earth continued to grow until his death in 1973. After Tolkien's passing, his son Christopher tirelessly edited and compiled his father's works. *The Silmarillion* was published in 1977, followed by *Unfinished Tales* in 1980, and ultimately the twelve-volume *History of Middle-earth* series was completed in 1996. Christopher Tolkien passed away in 2020 after several decades of faithful stewardship of his father's literary legacy.

The world of J. R. R. Tolkien has become arguably the most beloved fantasy world ever created; more than 100 million copies of *The Hobbit* have been sold worldwide as well as more than 150 million copies of *The Lord of the Rings*. Peter Jackson's adaptation trilogy of *The Lord of the Rings* earned seventeen Academy Awards, and *The Return of the King* was awarded eleven Oscars. These films changed the entertainment industry forever and brought fantasy into the forefront of popular culture. To this day, *The Lord of the Rings* remains present in the worldwide conversation as new adaptations of Tolkien's myth continue to unfold. Iterations such as Prime Video's *Rings of Power* and Warner Brothers' *War of the Rohirrim* tell new stories set within the familiar world of Tolkien, inviting viewers to explore different perspectives on Middle-earth. Tolkien's stories grow ever-deeper roots in the hearts of readers like you and me, and take on new dimensions through the vision of these creative projects. As Bilbo said to Frodo in Rivendell, "Someone else always has to carry on the story" (*LOTR*, Book II, ch. 1).

Tolkien the Hobbit

In a 1958 letter, Tolkien famously declared,

> I am in fact a hobbit (in all but size). I like gardens, trees and unmechanized farmlands; I smoke a pipe, and like good plain food (unrefrigerated), but detest French cooking; I like, and even dare to wear in these dull days, ornamental waistcoats. I am fond of mushrooms (out of a field); have a very simple sense of humour (which even my appreciative critics find tiresome); I go to bed late and get up late (when possible). I do not travel much. (*Letters*, 213)

It's easy to understand why the man who filled our hearts with tales of hobbits would identify with them. They enjoy simple pleasures, slow living, and treasure a good meal spent with friends above nearly everything else. While hobbits are, of course, not perfect—they are prone to gossip and are known to enjoy meddling, while also being altogether unwelcoming of any new ideas or people—they are rooted in a way of life that values "food and cheer and song above hoarded gold" (*The Hobbit*, ch. 18). Hobbits are a lovable people—and their stories within Tolkien's works provide endless inspiration for those of us who wish to adopt their way of life. They are, at the end of the day, the protagonists of our tale and the primary inspiration for this book.

Tolkien the Catholic

Tolkien holds a unique position in our culture as an author beloved by Christians and non-Christians alike. The communication of his religious philosophy through narrative has impacted readers so profoundly that some Catholics have advocated for the opening of his cause for canonization; at the same time, many nonreligious readers remain blissfully unaware that he was a religious person at all. His stories and themes are so universal that they speak to the heart of any reader, regardless of their faith or background.

I often joke that I think of Tolkien as my patron saint. This might surprise those unfamiliar with the Church's understanding of sainthood because certainly Tolkien was human and made mistakes. Catholics do not believe the saints themselves were infallible or perfect, however, but rather men and women who devoted themselves to God and pursued holiness until the end of their lives. Tolkien's devotion to his faith, as evidenced in his personal and professional life, can serve as inspiration for other Christians. His emphasis on hope, faith, and love were deeply rooted in the Gospel. While his works are undoubtedly beautiful and can be edifying for the spiritual life, it is important to recognize that neither Tolkien nor his works are infallible.

While the cause for Tolkien's canonization has not been officially opened, a prayer for private and personal use is available to be used by anyone interested. This prayer is included in appendix E, along with other prayers. I don't know if Tolkien will ever be recognized as a canonized saint, but I often ask for his intercession.

Is *The Lord of the Rings* a Catholic Story?

Any discussion of *The Lord of the Rings* must come with the inevitable disclaimer: This story was not intended to be interpreted as an allegory. Instead, Tolkien preferred applicability. He viewed allegory as "the purposed domination of the author," whereas applicability "resides in the freedom of the reader" (*LOTR*, 2nd ed., foreword). By inviting the reader to bring their own experience and interpretation to his works, Tolkien allowed his stories to grow beyond his own authorial intent. Any attempts at one-to-one comparison will fail because Tolkien's stories belong to themselves rather than to any real-world parallels. To attempt to derive direct allegory from *The*

Lord of the Rings is to neglect the whole of Tolkien's influences and will result in a flat understanding of the world we're entering into.

A reader may happily enjoy and understand *The Lord of the Rings* without the lens of Catholicism—millions have! In this book, you will not find the argument that a reader must be Catholic to understand Tolkien's stories. At the same time, I do believe *The Lord of the Rings* begins to take on a new depth of meaning when approached through a Catholic lens, one that both pierces the heart and edifies the soul. Therefore, we will tread this path together, seeking to unearth foundational elements of Tolkien's world while continuing, as Tolkien himself preferred, to preserve the freedom of the reader.

While he explained that his works were fundamentally religious and Catholic, he also emphasized that they were not allegorical. Tolkien didn't set out to evangelize via story—he simply set out to tell a good story. *The Lord of the Rings* doesn't need to lean on Catholicism as a crutch; instead, it can stand on its own as a classic work of literature. Tolkien believed a well-written fairy-story should include elements of moral and religious truth implicitly, without reference to the religion of the real or primary world. He felt a "fatal flaw" of the Arthurian legends was their explicit inclusion of Christianity within the myth. For this reason, you will not see churches and you will not meet Jesus in *The Lord of the Rings*. This sets Tolkien apart from many of his Christian contemporaries and allows for his work to serve as a bridge across which readers may venture into the perilous realms of both Faerie and faith if they feel called to.

Tolkien explained that he preferred to treat religion and theology as subtly as possible:

> I have purposely kept all allusions to the highest matters down to mere hints, perceptible only by the most attentive, or kept them under unexplained symbolic forms. So God and the "angelic" gods, the Lords or Powers of the West, only peep through in such places as Gandalf's conversation with Frodo: "Behind that there was something else at work, beyond any design of the Ring-maker's"; or in Faramir's Númenórean grace at dinner. (*Letters*, 156)

When it came to religion, almost all references were deliberately left out or removed from Middle-earth. The religious themes and symbolism were instead absorbed into the logic and world of the story itself (*Letters*, 131). We will not pretend Frodo equals Christ or that Sauron equals Satan. We can recognize, however, that there are elements of Christ's Passion interwoven into Frodo's journey and that the temptations of Sauron might remind Christians of Satan.

Tolkien wrote a story in which an unseen power guided all things in pursuit of goodness. Free will remained intact as a rule, but the thoughts or actions of characters would ultimately be woven into the grand schemes of Providence. While the God of this story could not be seen explicitly, he was always at work behind the scenes.

While Tolkien's faith was an integral part of his life and one of his primary inspirations, we must acknowledge that he drew inspiration from many other sources as well. A lifelong student of philology, or the study of language, Tolkien developed the languages of Middle-earth before he wrote the tales that would accompany them. He was fascinated by other bodies of mythology such as Anglo-Saxon, Finnish, Norse, and Greek. He had an abiding love for Old English poetry, *Beowulf* in particular. For example, the tragedy of Túrin Turambar was inspired by both the Finnish *Kalevala* and the Norse *Volsunga Saga*. The Downfall of Númenor was, in part, inspired by Plato's Atlantis. For a more thorough exploration of Tolkien's other influences, I have compiled a short list of recommended reading that can be found in appendix D.

How Should We Interpret Tolkien?

Fundamentally, there are two ways to read and understand literature. First, a reader may endeavor to interpret the work as they believe the author intended, framing the story within the author's own philosophy, historical context, and expressed intentions. This is often the most academic path. On the other hand, a reader may approach a work from their *own* unique perspective, weaving their personal experience, beliefs, and interpretations into the story as they understand it. In doing this, the reader forms a deeply personal connection to the story as it becomes a part of them.

While some argue one method is correct and the other is incorrect or even disrespectful, Tolkien allows his readers the freedom to do both. When interpreting Middle-earth, there is room to breathe. Framing a literary work within its context allows for a deeper understanding of its themes, characters, and overall messaging. This is the first step of doing literary analysis: We ask ourselves what the author intended, what elements of their lived experience shaped the story into what we are reading on the page, and what we believe their goals in writing the story were.

While this important part of literary analysis provides a strong foundation, we don't have to stop there. We can then turn inwardly and ask where we see ourselves in this story, how its characters reach out to us, and in what way this story may shape our own lives. We can enter into the story and allow ourselves to be changed by it while at the same time carrying the story into our own life. This symbiosis transforms both reader and story; the story begins to take on a life of its own beyond the text on the page. Just as the great myths live on in the retelling, we can carry these stories on with us.

How to Use This Book

Before we get ahead of ourselves, I want to acknowledge that Middle-earth can be daunting. There are so many characters, locations, and events within these stories that it can be easy to lose track of them all! Whether you are a casual fan or a longtime hobbit at heart, you may find yourself in need of clarifications or a refresher. Appendix A contains an overview of Tolkien's story world—from the creation of his universe to the major characters in the history of Middle-earth. That appendix also contains a synopsis of each of Tolkien's major works: *The Hobbit, The Lord of the Rings,* and *The Silmarillion.* For a primer on the key themes that are woven through Tolkien's writing, as well as an introduction to his ideas of eucatastrophe, sub-creation, and true myth, consult appendix B.

Each chapter in this book begins with a short epigraph from *The Hobbit* or *The Lord of the Rings*, loosely following the narrative from the Shire to Mordor and beyond. As we walk alongside Frodo and the other hobbits, we will delve into the various themes at play in the Legendarium and draw practical applications from each one.

We will start our journey in the same place *The Lord of the Rings* stories begin: in the Shire. The first few chapters of the book are focused on establishing a Shire of your own. Here, we will nestle ourselves into the cozy life of Hobbiton and make ourselves at home. We will explore the hallmarks of hobbit culture and seek to adopt these values into our own lives. At the same time, we will begin to explore the reality that hobbit life is not all strawberries and second breakfast: As we learn in *The Lord of the Rings*, a hobbit's life may require more courage, hope, and perseverance than anyone could guess. While we may be inspired by the idealized quaintness of the Shire, we can't overlook the hard-won lessons to be learned from the smallest folks of Middle-earth.

After we have firmly rooted ourselves in the truth, beauty, and goodness of our own Shire, later chapters in this book will help us branch out toward the world around us. A tree with strong roots may become a steadfast shelter, a beauty to behold, a source of shade, and a bounty of nourishing fruits. In a similar way, we should be striving for the betterment of the world around us. Just as Frodo had to leave the Shire to save Middle-earth, we too must look outside of ourselves in order to fulfill our own life's purpose. Which direction you travel is up to you to decide; it is my task to simply equip you with a map with which to take those first steps.

At the end of chapter 1, I introduce a list of values embodied by Tolkien's heroes. Each chapter will focus on four of these values, exploring the ways that they have been nurtured and supported in Middle-earth. Along the journey, we will also examine the way Tolkien's own life shaped Middle-earth, as well as meet saints and biblical figures who exemplified these values. These insights are intended as a way to draw the lessons of Middle-earth out of the fictional world and into our own.

Each chapter will close with a reflection prompt called "The Road Goes On," which might give you ideas for personal growth and action. By the end of our time together, we will have entered into Tolkien's stories and returned home with a new perspective, inspired and strengthened for our own adventures ahead. We will have identified which values of Middle-earth resonate with us and begun to cultivate a life that supports, nourishes, and defends these values. We will have deepened our understanding and appreciation for both Tolkien's fictional world and our own reality. We will have rooted ourselves in beauty, goodness, and truth with feet firmly on the ground of both Middle-earth and our own neighborhood.

I hope this book helps you draw on Tolkien's wisdom to become who you were created to be. I'll be with you every step of the way. Are you ready?

Chapter 1

ESTABLISH YOUR SHIRE

Values: Harmony, Belonging, Mirth, and Wonder

> In a hole in the ground there lived a hobbit. Not a nasty, dirty, wet hole, filled with the ends of worms and an oozy smell, nor yet a dry, bare, sandy hole with nothing in it to sit down on or to eat: it was a hobbit-hole, and that means comfort.
>
> *The Hobbit*, ch. 1

The sun is setting behind the hills of Hobbiton. The light fades on one of the last days of summer and wind rustles the first leaves of fall from the trees. A small crowd has gathered at the local inn to discuss something of special magnificence. Indeed, in just a few days, the Shire will be treated to a shared birthday party for Bilbo Baggins and his nephew Frodo. Conversation and speculation flow as freely as ale from the tap, and the fire on the hearth burns long into the evening.

The Shire was a humble place to live; its inhabitants were mostly common folk who preferred a garden shovel to a sword. They lived in tight-knit communities, minding the business of their neighbors as well as their own. They were a small and unobtrusive people who dwelt in harmony with the earth and valued simplicity and peace over consuming power. Their days were filled with hard yet rewarding work, and their evenings were spent with simple hearty meals shared with friends and family. In many ways, the life of a hobbit was idyllic—and Tolkien wrote it this way intentionally.

The Lord of the Rings does not rush its story; instead, it lingers in the Shire for as long as possible. Tolkien painted a detailed picture of hobbit life at the beginning of *The Lord of the Rings*. In its prologue, we learn the history and culture of the halfling, and we spend the first several chapters within the borders of the Shire as we learn about a meeting of the minds, a party of special magnificence, and a group of friends who will soon be swept off onto the road together. Tolkien spends so much time here to nourish the reader in goodness and create the same resiliency in readers that hobbits will soon need to utilize. In doing this, we can grow to love the Shire as much as Frodo did and begin to understand what he was willing to lose in order to save it.

While hobbits were known mostly for being soft and unassuming and preferring life's simpler pleasures, they were also surprisingly resilient and able to forgo the comforts of home when necessary. Others marveled at their ability to resist temptation and despair, a virtue that can largely be attributed to the wholesome nature of life in Hobbiton. As we begin our journey through Middle-earth, and start building a life that reflects the best parts of the Shire, it is only fitting that we begin in the same place as *The Lord of the Rings* does: in a hole in the ground, where there lived a hobbit.

Entering into Hobbit Life

Imagine you've purchased a home on Bagshot Row: You're moving into the Shire! What will you expect? What will life look like? Your home might feel empty at first with boxes piled up along the walls and little by way of furniture, but it will soon be filled with the bustling everyday life of a hobbit. There will be a time for toil and rest and everything in between. Imagine a hearty second breakfast that nourishes the body as well as the soul when shared with friends and family. Warm drinks and conversation enjoyed before the glow of the fireplace, songs that fill the heart with memories and joy, and gifts given with thought and generosity. Hobbits did not rush themselves from one task to another; rather, they savored the joy of each moment. They had a peace to them that was deeply rooted and steadfast.

For thousands of years prior to the events of *The Hobbit*, their very existence had been largely overlooked by the rest of the world. They minded their own business and contributed little to the grand histories of the world—well, that is, until Fate would bring them into one of history's greatest tales. They were the most unlikely of all creatures to become entangled in the War of the Ring, and yet it was through their humility, groundedness, and courage that Middle-earth was ultimately saved. A curious premise to found a story upon, don't you think?

The Virtues of the Shire

Hobbits were fond of slow-cooking, simple meals, hosting, gift giving, letter writing, songs and poetry, walking and hiking, fishing, gardening, and gathering around the fireside. They were not as hardy as dwarves nor as beautiful as elves, but they were good-natured and bright-eyed and possessed many strengths and skills often overlooked or forgotten by others.

Hobbits were not infallible or unfallen. Indeed, some hobbits were quite nasty and even cooperated with evil. Just like us, hobbits had to choose goodness. And even the best of hobbits were not perfect—they were prone to gossip, closed-mindedness, and the occasional bouts of scheming. But it is in their "everyday-ness" that we learn how a life of simplicity and virtue is possible. Though hobbits did not claim vast wealth or power, their lives were nonetheless rich in other ways. They may be seen by others as humble or lowly, but their hearts and homes were bursting with beauty, truth, and goodness. The secret to a happy hobbit was not in jewels or gold but in a rich interior life. A person's interior life is essentially the life of one's soul. It is built of habits, rhythms, routines, and disciplines that all work together to form you as a person. The interior life is a foundation and guide for your exterior, or outward, life. Just as a seed sprouts into a great tree, your interior life is at the core of who you are. Establishing a Shire of our own may be outwardly expressed through crafts, recipes, or décor, but it is first done by cultivating a healthy interior life.

In her spiritual memoir, *The Interior Castle*, St. Teresa of Avila wrote of the soul as if it were a castle. If we are to take this principle and look at it through a Middle-earth-tinted lens, we might then say our soul is like a hobbit hole. Or a dwarven cavern, an elven city, or whatever you might choose. In this chapter, we will be laying the foundation for our interior lives based on the values and virtues of Hobbiton, and we'll do so using these distinctive elements of hobbit culture: food, cheer, and song; giving ourselves space for quiet reflection; and living in tune with the natural seasons.

Food and Cheer and Song

The last words of Thorin Oakenshield praised the simple life of Hobbiton. As he lay dying after the Battle of Five Armies, he said to Bilbo, "There is more in you of good than you know, child of the kindly West. Some courage and some wisdom, blended in measure. If more of us valued food and cheer and song above hoarded gold, it would be a merrier world" (*The Hobbit,* ch. 18). Much like Thorin, I find myself admiring the "food and cheer and song" of hobbit life. His words are a testament to the beauty of an ordinary life, and these three elements are a good place to start when examining the virtues of the Shire.

Hobbits were always hungry. In fact, they would enjoy six meals a day as often as possible. These meals were often eaten as a community, whether in the common room of an inn or at home with company. They preferred simple foods, as an array of food would need to be stored throughout the seasons and available for parties both expected and unexpected. For example, Bilbo Baggins's pantry was stocked well enough to feed thirteen dwarves and one wizard when they showed up out of the blue. The dwarves' requests included raspberry jam and apple tart, mince pies and cheese, pork pie, salad, cakes, ale, coffee, eggs, cold chicken, and pickles. Later at Bilbo's 111th birthday party, his guests were treated to a legendary feast. Bilbo had been "specializing in food for many years and his table had a high reputation," and partygoers were not disappointed (*LOTR*, Book I, ch. 1). For hobbits, food was more than just fuel—it was an opportunity for connection, the sharing of culture, an invitation to love, and a source of comfort.

Hobbits were good-natured and possessed a tendency toward optimism that would carry them through seasons of difficulty. They were prone to burst out into song without any warning or care, even in very inconvenient or dangerous times. Mirth, an outpouring of gladness often heard through laughter, was a defining characteristic of hobbits. Their laughter was an almost inalienable quality and one of their strengths.

The power of mirth was not confined to the Shire. When tempted by Frodo's offer of the One Ring, Galadriel responded by laughing "with a sudden clear laugh" (*LOTR*, Book II, ch. 7). When Saruman attempted to seduce Gandalf to his side with the spell of his voice, Gandalf laughed, causing the fantasy to vanish like a puff of smoke. When the hosts of Aragorn came forth into battle out of the Paths of the Dead, Tolkien wrote, "The mirth of the Rohirrim was a torrent of laughter and a flashing of swords, and the joy and wonder of the City was a music of trumpets and a ringing of bells" (*LOTR*, Book V, ch. 6). When the Witch-king of Angmar declared to Éowyn that no living man might hinder him, Éowyn responded with laughter and defiance. When Sam awoke in the Field of Cormallen after the destruction of the Ring, he was overcome with emotion and ultimately burst into bewildered laughter.

Laughter produces a clarity that pierces through shadow and deception. Mirth cannot be feigned but is instead the true nature of a heart that has clung to hope and found strength in doing so. Cultivating joy is one of our best defenses against despair.

The Apostle of Joy, Philip Neri

Tolkien's formative years were guided by a saint who was known for being a person of good cheer. On Christmas day of 1903, following his mother's conversion in 1900, the young John Ronald was received into the Catholic Church at the Birmingham Oratory. It was then that he took St. Philip Neri as his confirmation saint; because Neri had founded the Congregation of the Oratory more than three hundred years earlier, it was a natural and fitting choice.

During his lifetime, Philip Neri was known for his gentle and friendly disposition and would later be called "the Apostle of Joy." One anecdote recalls that he had a mystical experience that caused him to nearly die of laughter; when he did ultimately die, it was discovered that his heart had grown too large for his ribcage. Neri instilled a charism of mirth within the religious community that founded the oratory, and this culture of joy would be integral to Tolkien's childhood. After the death of his mother, the young John Ronald drew on Neri's legacy of steadfast joy as a defense against sorrow and grief, equipping him for the trials of the years to come.

Poetry and Song

I'm embarrassed to admit that I used to skip the songs and poems when reading Tolkien. Always in a hurry to move along with the story, I saw them as tedious at best and altogether obnoxious at worst. But as I have continued to study Tolkien, I have learned that often the heart of the story is contained within these songs. Song for Tolkien is not merely flowery dialogue or exposition strung into verse—it is integral to the story as a whole.

In fact, in the very beginning of his Legendarium, Tolkien's world itself was created through song. The Ainulindalë, the Music of the Ainur, tells of the creation of the world through music under the direction of the supreme God Eru Ilúvatar. It is said in *The Silmarillion* that the echoes of this music can be heard in water. The elves therefore considered water the dearest of all elements, a testament to their love of music.

Song was also prevalent in Bilbo's adventures. When Bilbo met the dwarves, their song of misty mountains and lost treasure swept him away into their culture and history and endeared them to him. He became invested in their story because of their song.

Years after Bilbo's journey had ended, Frodo and his friends were on a journey of their own. In the Old Forest, they met the enigmatic Tom Bombadil. The songs of Tom Bombadil held a curious power within their words. His voice was able to command both Old Man Willow and Barrow-wight alike. While Tom Bombadil's nature was intentionally left unexplained, some have theorized he was the embodiment of the music of the Ainur. (I'm quite fond of this idea, myself!)

Days later, Frodo and his friends followed Strider through the wilderness to Rivendell. Along the road, Sam surprised them by reciting a verse about the elven king Gil-galad. He explained that Bilbo had taught him the song, though he did not remember the whole thing. In a hobbit society that was largely illiterate, songs were a powerful way of passing down history.

On this same journey, Aragorn recounted the tale of Beren and Lúthien to the hobbits through song, weaving an image in their minds more effectively than if he had told it plainly. During the quest of Beren and Lúthien, Finrod, the brother of Galadriel, was captured by Sauron. During his captivity, Finrod and Sauron strove against one another in songs of power. Ultimately, the song of Sauron was more powerful than Finrod's and the elf fell before him.

Sauron, who was himself a participant in the music of the Ainur, would have been well versed in the power of music. The verse inscribed on Sauron's Ring, and the full poem that accompanies it, can also be seen as a song. Much like song and myth, language itself has been passed down through generations and with it comes history. As a philologist, Tolkien was fascinated by the way the two were inextricably linked, especially in light of oral tradition.

Songs were also used to announce important moments in Middle-earth history, such as when the great eagles brought news of Sauron's downfall to the people of Gondor. Similarly, the tale of Frodo was recounted in song to those present in the Field of Cormallen after the destruction of the Ring.

Much like in Middle-earth, song holds an important place in our own world. Songs can tell stories, communicate themes and lessons, and pass down history. Song can preserve cultural memory far after history books have been lost or forgotten, serving as a link between generations. Song can be a source of communal expression, drawing people together in harmony and shared experience. It can also be a source of personal expression, as feelings, beliefs, or stories may be communicated more easily in song than in the spoken word.

The music of Middle-earth has deepened my appreciation for the role music plays in my own life. I often find myself humming Tolkien's songs or reflecting on the importance of their themes in our own world. The stories told by film and television adaptations of Tolkien's works have been enriched by their accompanying musical scores; I have been particularly moved by the music of Howard Shore (*The Lord of the Rings* and *The Hobbit* trilogies) and Bear McCreary (*The Rings of Power* series). These musical compositions have served as a bridge between fiction and reality, stirring my heart to joy, sorrow, and every emotion in between.

Meditation and Contemplation

The quiet and contemplative life of the hobbit was quite different from our busy, often cacophonous modern lives. There was a slowness that was secure in itself, a patience and willingness to "waste" time that I find admirable. While hobbits did not specifically pray or intentionally meditate, they made room in their lives for quiet, mental rest, and reflection.

Carrying this value into our own modern setting, we can be reminded to seek out time for quiet contemplation or meditation. In a religious context, prayer and meditation are at the heart of the spiritual life. In appendix E, I have included the text of several prayers that Tolkien himself recommended to his son. Many Catholics find solace in the prayers of the Rosary, which are all sourced from scripture. These prayers were so meaningful and familiar to Tolkien that he even translated many of them into his elvish languages, though there is no reason to believe that he actually prayed in elvish.

Cooperation with Nature and the Seasons

Hobbits lived in harmony with the natural rhythms of the seasons. Certain crops were harvested at certain times, spring brought rain and winter delivered snow, and so forth. For us, it was not until recent generations that people widely departed from routines that were dictated by the seasons of nature. While there is certainly security and comfort to be found in abundance, there is also something lost when the connection to and dependence on the land is broken. Tolkien's villains strove to dominate the natural rhythms of the earth and distort the natural order of life. Hobbits, by contrast, embraced it.

In the spring, we plant our gardens, and in the summer and autumn we harvest them. Spring and summer bring long days in the sunshine, and autumn and winter bring nights spent indoors. Connecting our lives more closely to natural rhythms can be as simple as pulling out the warm clothes at the end of autumn and packing them away in spring; or adjusting meal plans according to which foods are in season. These small acts of cooperating with the seasons reinforce our connection to the natural, created world. You are probably already doing this more than you realize, but here are a few other ways to be intentional about connecting our lives to the natural world.

Routines and Rhythms

Routines and rhythms were very important to hobbit life. Being late for dinner was considered one of the worst possible outcomes of an adventure; Gandalf was widely regarded as a nuisance in the Shire because of his tendency to disrupt their cultural status quo with his new ideas and proposals of adventure.

In pursuit of hobbit-like consistency, I have found it incredibly grounding and fruitful to intentionally establish routines and fall into step with them—but it hasn't been easy. Anyone who knows me has noticed that creating rhythms within my life is one of my biggest struggles. I quickly lose track of habits or to-do lists and often find my life feeling untethered and out of control. In this regard, I am a constant work-in-progress. The simplest way that I have been able to reign in this sense of chaos is to begin with anchoring my life in the recurring events of my calendar. These range from the mundane (the trash is collected every Monday) to the more large-scale (Christmas is on December 25). I keep these hard dates down on my calendar and then structure the rest of my life around them.

Establishing habits and systems in our lives will reduce mental clutter and make room for creativity, love, and peace to flourish. Because of the rhythms and routines I establish for myself, I have more time and space to love those around me. When my monthly, weekly, or daily schedules have necessary tasks or events automatically built in, it is easier to accommodate the unexpected without falling behind on the non-negotiables.

The Liturgical Calendar

If you are a member of a religious tradition, your community may have a calendar of its own. As a Catholic, I have found so much stability in the Church's liturgical calendar. The Catholic liturgical calendar begins each new year with Advent, as winter approaches, and follows with the feast of Christmas. Similarly, the season of Lent precedes the joyful celebration of Easter. There are also periods of Ordinary Time throughout the year, which are filled with various smaller feasts and traditions.

I have found that following these patterns in my own life provides stability and connects me to something greater than myself: my faith community. Tolkien himself observed this calendar and even incorporated some important dates from it in *The Lord of the Rings,* most notably December 25 (Christmas—the day the Fellowship of the Ring departs from Rivendell) and March 25 (the Annunciation—the day on which the One Ring is destroyed).

If you are a student or parent of a student, much of your life follows an academic calendar; if you are a sports fan, you may align your schedule with sports seasons or certain matches; countries and cultures have their own days of remembrance and celebration as well. I recommend taking out a calendar and mapping out the major events of your life so you can develop your rhythms around them. You get to decide what moments in the year are important to you, and planning ahead for them allows you to enter them more fully. Without this kind of intentionality, life gets too busy and suddenly you look up and years have passed.

While you have your calendar out, add these two important Tolkienian dates: Tolkien Reading Day on March 25 and Hobbit Day on September 22. More about both of these important dates can be found in appendix C.

Becoming a Hobbit at Heart

Now that we have explored the dispositions at the core of hobbit culture, we can begin to bring some of them into our own life. We can start building a home environment that reflects our values, which will create a strong foundation for the journey ahead. Which aspects of hobbit life resonate with you? Branching out toward Tolkien's other heroes, are there any you admire? When thinking about your life, what values do you want to cultivate?

Becoming a hobbit at heart is less about eating second breakfast or wearing ornamental waistcoats and more about adopting a mindset that guides your decisions and your path. I like to think of life in Hobbiton as a sort of metaphorical childhood for Tolkien's heroes, especially Frodo Baggins. It is within the safety and confines of the Shire that he is nourished, educated, and equipped with everything he needs for the journey Fate will demand of him.

Much like how life in the Shire is presented as a foundation for the rest of Frodo's story, your interior life is a foundation for the rest of *your* story. This is the time to take stock of what you value and create an environment for yourself that nourishes the values that are important to you—because leaving the Shire is a dangerous business.

THE ROAD GOES ON

Choose five to ten of the following values that you would like to incorporate more into your life and write them down in a notebook. Keep them in mind as we move forward with this book. You can also download a printable worksheet of these hobbit values from www.avemariapress.com/pages/into-the-heart-of-middle-earth-resources.

Hobbit Values:

Adaptability
Adventure
Altruism
Authenticity
Availability
Belonging
Bravery
Clarity
Clemency
Community
Connection
Consolation
Conviction
Courage
Detachment
Devotion
Discernment
Empowerment
Faith
Fellowship
Firmness
Foresight
Fortitude
Generosity
Groundedness
Growth
Harmony
Hope
Hospitality
Humility
Justice
Leadership
Mercy
Mirth
Optimism
Peace
Perseverance
Provision
Purpose, Resolution
Resourcefulness
Respect
Rootedness
Sacrifice
Simplicity
Steadiness
Stewardship
Stillness
Stoutness of Heart
Surrender
Temperance
Tookishness
Trust
Unbrokenness
Understanding
Wonder

Chapter 2

Open the Door to Providence

Values: Rootedness, Tookishness, Authenticity, and Adventure

> Then something Tookish woke up inside him, and he wished to go and see the great mountains, and hear the pine-trees and the waterfalls, and explore the caves, and wear a sword instead of a walking-stick.
>
> *The Hobbit*, ch. 1

One day at teatime, a company of dwarves floods through the front door of Bag End with an offer of adventure, and suddenly the comfortable life of Bilbo Baggins is changed forever. Suddenly the vast world has been opened up to him, and he is presented with a choice he had never before considered. Bilbo is suddenly at war within himself, his Tookish desire for adventure threatening to override his Baggins-ish common sense.

As the son of Belladonna Took and Bungo Baggins, Bilbo came from two very different families. Where the Bagginses were predictable and had an aversion to adventure, the Tooks were unpredictable and drawn to it. Suddenly, with an opportunity presented by Fate, Bilbo realized he was ready for a change. This moment would mark the beginning of a new era for him; he finds himself being swept off on an adventure. Along the way, he would fully become himself, both Baggins and Took.

Each of us has been created with a purpose. Some may feel that we understand this purpose from an early age, while others may spend a lifetime in its pursuit. There is no one-size-fits-all answer to the question of who we were meant to be or what we were born to do, but there are concrete steps we can take to discern our path. The first step, which may be the scariest, is simply to open your heart to Providence. Leave room for the unexpected party; if something "Tookish" awakens in you, listen to it.

Fate Calls, We Answer

Fate often arrives in unexpected ways, but if we are willing to open the door to opportunity, these promptings can help us to become who we were meant to be. Fate may make itself known in the form of our own talents or aspirations, in the understanding of our heritage, in the reception of a gift, or, in Bilbo's case, in the arrival of a company of dwarves upon his doorstep.

For Bilbo, Gandalf acted as an instrument of Fate when he suggested Bilbo for the role of burglar in the quest that defines the story of *The Hobbit*. Though Gandalf was the guide, it was ultimately Bilbo himself who took those first steps out of his door. And when the Ring happened across his path, it was Bilbo who picked it up. The same call came decades later as the leaders of Middle-earth each felt individually prompted to travel to Rivendell for counsel. Fate has a way of bringing people together in order for them to act; these promptings are ultimately calling these characters toward goodness. Just as each member of the Council of Elrond was called together, Fate calls to each of us and we need only answer.

While Bilbo did not go out seeking adventure—in fact, he was actively avoiding it when Gandalf first came to visit—he did ultimately open the door and step out onto the road. None of the great tales of Middle-earth would have happened if their heroes were not willing to step out of their comfort zones and place one foot in front of the other to set out into the unknown. Whether we are embarking upon our own spiritual journey or an actual physical one, we can be inspired by Tolkien's examples.

As much as we love the Shire, we can't stay there forever! The great tales of the world are not told within the four walls of our comfort and security but rather outside of them, beneath the wild night sky and across the vastness of the earth. We are molded in the Shire, but we are truly forged on the road to Mount Doom. The virtues of the Shire should not remain hidden away or be forgotten on our journey, as though we have left it completely behind. Rather, we carry the Shire with us wherever the road may lead.

Gandalf as a Spiritual Guide

While he was branded a "disturber of the peace" by the residents of Hobbiton, Gandalf was truly a *servant* of peace (*LOTR*, Book I, ch. 1). His primary work was in guiding the free peoples of Middle-earth toward goodness and light, always in opposition to evil. We too can serve as instruments of Fate, if we follow Gandalf's example and build our lives around faithfulness and service.

In a loose sense, Gandalf can be seen as a spiritual guide for the protagonists of both *The Hobbit* and *The Lord of the Rings*. He offered his insight, wisdom, and advice without seeking to override the free will of anyone. He could have forced Bilbo to surrender the Ring just as easily as he could have picked Frodo up and carried him all the way to Rivendell. He could have taken the Ring away from Bilbo or Frodo to keep for himself as easily as taking candy from a baby, but that was not Gandalf's way. When Gandalf came to Middle-earth at the beginning of the Third Age, he was entrusted with Narya, one of the three elven rings of power. Its original bearer, the elvish shipwright Círdan, gave it to him saying, "Take now this Ring, for thy labours and thy cares will be heavy, but in all it will support thee and defend thee from weariness. For this is the Ring of Fire, and herewith, maybe, thou shalt rekindle hearts to the valour of old in a world that grows chill" (*Silm*, Of the Rings of Power and the Third Age). Círdan foresaw that Gandalf's quest would be of extraordinary importance. This ring's unique powers spoke to rekindle weary hearts in the fight against Sauron. Gandalf was one of the five wizards, the Istari, who were sent to Middle-earth "to encourage and bring out the native powers of the Enemies of Sauron" (*Letters*, 144). In the end, Gandalf was the only one who remained faithful to this task. He did not seek out lordship or dominion of the peoples of Middle-earth as Saruman did, but instead sought only to prompt those who would resist Sauron to action. It was not meant for Gandalf alone to defeat Sauron, but for Gandalf to aid and guide those who would take up arms against evil.

In his fight against the Balrog in Moria, Gandalf proclaimed that he was a servant of the Secret Fire. The Secret Fire, also called the Flame Imperishable, was set into the heart of the world at its creation. This power could be commanded by Eru alone, and only through it could new life be made. In *Tolkien and The Silmarillion*, author Clyde Kilby recounts Tolkien explaining that the "Secret Fire sent to burn at the heart of the world in the beginning was the Holy Spirit" (59).

In the Christian tradition, the Holy Spirit is the third person of the Holy Trinity who advocates for and guides people toward goodness and truth. In this context, we can think of Gandalf as a servant of the Holy Spirit, guiding the peoples of Middle-earth with a singular purpose toward goodness. Whereas the Secret Fire remains fictional, the Holy Spirit is real and present in our lives and functions in a similar way. In adopting Gandalf's commitment to service, we can also guide those around us toward goodness.

An Encouraging Thought

After Bilbo's disappearance, everything he owned was passed down to his heir and nephew Frodo, including his magic, golden Ring. As Gandalf later revealed the nature and history of this Ring, Frodo began to understand that he had found himself in a situation far greater and more perilous than he had imagined. Ultimately, he resolved to leave the Shire and carry this Ring to Rivendell where its fate could be decided. Frodo felt overwhelmed and ill-equipped for this task. After all, he was just one small hobbit. Gandalf encouraged Frodo, explaining, "Behind that there was something else at work, beyond any design of the Ring-maker. I can put it no plainer than by saying that Bilbo was meant to find the Ring, and not by its maker. In which case you were also meant to have it. And that may be an encouraging thought" (*LOTR*, Book I, ch. 2).

Gandalf's encouragement may seem counterintuitive; rather than insisting Frodo was chosen because of his own strength or abilities, he did the opposite. When Frodo asked Gandalf why he was chosen to bear the burden of the Ring, Gandalf responded, "You may be sure that it was not for any merit that others do not possess: not for power or wisdom, at any rate. But you have been chosen, and you must therefore use such strength and heart and wits as you have" (*LOTR*, Book I, ch. 2).

Frodo did not find any of this encouraging, lamenting that he felt he had so few of these traits. And yet he still agreed to go forward. Frodo's journey began with a complete reliance on Providence; he was keenly aware that he himself did not possess the merit to accomplish this task himself. At the same time, he was still willing to pour as much strength, heart, and wits into the journey as he had. Gandalf understood more than anyone that Fate had a way of weaving itself in the most unexpected patterns, and in Frodo's smallness, the designs of Providence would be made visible.

Providence is also at work in our world now as much as it was in Middle-earth. Like Frodo and Bilbo, we have each been created and chosen for some purpose. Gandalf used language that spoke to a higher power at work when consoling Frodo: You were *chosen*. You were *called*. You were *meant*. These are all words that acknowledge Providence at work, and they are just as true for us as they were for Frodo—we need only respond to what they awaken in us.

At the Council of Elrond, Frodo came to accept that he had been entrusted with the Ring for a purpose. Frodo marveled to hear his own words volunteering to carry it to Mordor, as if some other will was guiding his small voice. "'I will take the Ring,' he said, 'though I do not know the way'" (*LOTR*, Book II, ch. 2). This decision was rooted in trust and humility, virtues that would lay the foundation for the rest of the trials to come.

Tolkien's heroes often wrestled with loneliness, uncertainty, or even feeling like a burden. This is something I find deeply relatable, and you might, too. Merry felt like "baggage" amidst the proud and valiant warriors of Rohan, a feeling underscored after one of the warriors tripped over him as he sat on the ground. Afterward, the warrior even referred to him as "Master Bag" (*LOTR*, Book V, ch. 5). Pippin also wrestled with these same feelings, worrying whether he should've remained home. Even Elrond himself initially resisted the idea of the two young hobbits joining the Fellowship of the Ring at all.

These examples bring me great comfort when I am feeling ill-suited for the tasks of my life, however big or small. If it weren't for the heroic actions of Merry and Pippin, the fate of many others would have been far worse. None of us will ever truly know the full impact of our life while we are still living it. And even the "smallest" of us can make a big difference when we are pursuing our calling. In becoming who we were meant to be, we can rekindle hearts and set the world ablaze.

"The Mission of My Life"

St. John Henry Newman has an interesting connection to Tolkien. He was a prominent 1800s Oxford priest who began his ministry as an Anglican and later converted to Catholicism. In a time when England was both culturally and legally discriminatory toward Catholicism, his conversion caused widespread scandal. Just as it later happened for Tolkien's mother, Mabel, Newman's personal relationships and professional reputation suffered because of his religious beliefs.

Yet despite knowing the risk, he followed his convictions. After being ordained a priest in the Roman Catholic rite in 1846, he joined the Congregation of the Oratory. This congregation had been founded three centuries earlier by St. Philip Neri, Tolkien's Confirmation saint. Newman founded the Birmingham Oratory in 1848, the first Oratory to be established in the English-speaking world. He died in 1890, just two years before Tolkien's birth; he was beatified on September 19, 2010, and was canonized on October 13, 2019.

Newman believed that God had created him for a distinct and unique purpose. In "The Mission of My Life," he wrote,

> God has created me to do him some definite service. He has committed some work to me which he has not committed to another. I have my mission. I may never know it in this life, but I shall be told it in the next. I am a link in a chain, a bond of connection between persons. He has not created me for naught. I shall do good; I shall do his work.

Even after leaving Birmingham, Tolkien would continue to be influenced by Newman's legacy. Fr. Francis Morgan, Tolkien's "second father," served as a close friend and personal secretary of Newman at the Oratory. In their time together, Fr. Francis may have imparted some of Newman's wisdom to Tolkien or shared about his experiences with the holy priest. In Oxford, Tolkien was active in the Oration community, often attending the Oratory parish, St. Aloysius; Tolkien was also a member of the Newman Society both in Oxford and on a national level. Newman's spiritual biography, *Apologia Pro Vita Sua*, is included in the library of books Tolkien read, consulted, bought, or borrowed in his lifetime.

Refracted Light

Tolkien echoed Newman's affirmation of individual purpose and dignity in "Mythopoeia." In this poem, Tolkien describes humanity as "the refracted Light through whom is splintered from a single white to many hues, and endlessly combined." God, the source of all creation, is presented as a single white light. Each one of us is a uniquely refracted hue in an endless sea of colors.

As a child, I remember being enchanted by the rainbows that would appear on the walls or floors of my grandparents' home when the light would hit their sun-catching prisms in just the right way. I would lie on the soft warm carpet of their living room and marvel at the way the colors would dance across my hands when I tried to hold the rainbow. I wondered at the way the light of the sun could shine through the crystal to produce so many different colors, each color making its neighbor seem more beautiful.

Following this symbolism, each of us bears our own unique mission—a distinct hue that enriches and beautifies the world. Without your hue, the beauty of the world is diminished and its work left unfinished. There has never been anyone exactly like you, and there never will be again. Each of us is meant for something—we each have a purpose. The world is enriched by your existence. Sometimes you might not feel like this is true, but the light shines whether you believe in it or not.

From an early age, Tolkien recognized his passions and pursued them wholeheartedly. His love for language led him to invent several of his own as well as to become an esteemed professor of philology; his love for mythology led him to create his own world and an entire multi-thousand-year history to go alongside it. He also didn't force himself to choose one interest over the other but instead pursued both myth and language in earnest. He didn't settle for mediocrity, and neither should we. There can be so much pressure to carefully curate a personal brand for ourselves, lest we are left behind or forgotten. Especially in the digital world, there can be a temptation to shrink ourselves into something neat and tidy and marketable. Instead, Tolkien encourages us to be ourselves fully. Like Bilbo, there are many different facets to each of us—we all have "Baggins" and "Tookish" sides—and we should honor each of them. Bilbo's acceptance of both sides of his heritage reveals a person who is at peace with himself. By contrast, Gollum is at war internally, constantly arguing aloud with himself.

Each of us brings a new perspective to the world. We each come from different heritages and upbringings with different tendencies, trades, skills, and traditions. While each individual can be perceived as a distinct hue within the vast spectrum of human existence, we all possess the full spectrum of human potential within us.

We have spent these first two chapters cultivating an environment that supports our own values as inspired by the beauty, truth, and goodness of the Shire. Next, we will shift into a discussion of the "little way" of the halfling, a life of trust, humility, and surrender. As we continue to form our interior life around our values, we are building a foundation for the rest of our lives and equipping ourselves for wherever the road might lead.

THE ROAD GOES ON

While reflecting on the core values you chose in chapter 1, think about the things that make you unique: your heritage, memories, family, interests, hobbies, skills, perspectives, etc. What connections do you see between the values you chose and your unique background? Why do you think you landed on the values you chose? What do they say about who you aspire to be?

Chapter 3

DISCOVER THE LITTLE WAY

Values: Humility, Surrender, Simplicity, and Trust

> This is the hour of the Shire-folk, when they arise from their quiet fields to shake the towers and counsels of the Great.
>
> *LOTR*, Book II, ch. 2

Seventy-seven years after Bilbo's mysterious disappearance, Frodo has finally set off on an adventure of his own. He has sold Bag End to the Sackville-Baggins and, by all appearances, is beginning a new chapter of life in Crickhollow. But unbeknownst to his neighbors, Fate has set his true path much farther east, and with each step Frodo takes away from home he wonders if he will ever see the Shire again. Before him lie many miles of unknown road, yet neither Frodo nor his companions will turn aside. Though none of these hobbits fully understand their peril, they each take a deep breath, adjust their pack, and prepare to be swept off onto the road wherever it may lead.

For the hobbits, the world beyond the Shire was largely a blank map. In accepting his role as Ring bearer, Frodo was plunging himself into a world unknown. We might look at Frodo's journey in hindsight and feel like we would never be able to do something so brave or monumental, but we forget that he began with one simple yes. One step out of his door. Then another. Then another.

Similarly, we need only take one step at a time, one yes at a time. While our own journeys might not seem as big or important as Frodo's, it is in these small daily moments of trust and surrender that we will grow to become who we were meant to be. As the distance between himself and his home grew, so did Frodo's courage and commitment to his quest. Together, we will explore the unwavering trust of hobbits so as to emulate them.

Hobbits were resilient to evil, in part, because they came from such a wholesome environment. Gandalf remarked with wonder that he believed some hobbits would resist the Ring for far longer than others might think, and in the end, he was proven right.. The heart of a hobbit was vibrant, radiating warmth and a sense of true belonging. It was a log fire crackling in the hearth. It was a song that filled the room with memory, gratitude, hope, and joy. It was a gift given with care and generosity, a treasure of jewels hidden beneath roots and grass. It was steadfast, a shelter from the storm. And it was unyielding because it had deep roots that could weather long winters.

The journey of a hobbit was one of complete trust: to step out onto the road without counting the cost. Despite shadow and doubt, they plodded on, driven by the hope that each step would carry them toward an end that they could not yet see. When the strength of man, elf, and dwarf faltered, it was the quiet fortitude of the hobbit that saved Middle-earth.

Many of the wise overlooked the hobbit: a small thing, short and round and simple. They were a humble people, preferring their gardens and kitchens to castles and fortresses. Most hobbits were unbothered by the happenings of the wide world around them, content to mind their own business (and the business of their relatives) without any news from the world beyond their borders. In the great histories of Middle-earth, the hobbit may have existed as no more than a footnote. That is, until our story begins.

Defending the Shire

Many people want to imagine being a hobbit at heart as sitting around eating strawberries in the grass, but they often forget how hard-won those strawberries are. Everyone wants to eat second breakfast and spend time with their friends, but nobody wants to carry Sauron's Ring to Mordor. We think of hobbits as quaint and twee, but there is strength hidden within them that would rival the greatest elf-lord. There is grit and courage and many things beyond. Sometimes being a hobbit at heart means running out the door without a handkerchief because adventure is calling. Other times it means carrying a burden much greater than you think you can bear, not because you think so highly of yourself but because you know it has been asked of you.

The year after the Ring was destroyed brought the most bountiful harvest the Shire had seen for generations, but it was not without cost. The residents of Hobbiton were able to enjoy their food and cheer and song because they collectively worked hard and prioritized community over profit or individualism. Hobbits were keenly aware of their duty to one another as well as to the land they lived upon. They took great interest (sometimes too much) in the affairs of their neighbor and were more than willing to inconvenience themselves to help them. They also farmed the earth diligently without ravaging it. It is also worth noting that Frodo felt a love for both the land of the Shire itself and its people, but not in a nationalistic sense; he did not want to save the Shire to the detriment of other realms, but desired peace throughout all of Middle-earth.

The safety of the Shire was never guaranteed. Instead, it was something hard-won by those who protected and defended it. In *The Fellowship of the Ring*, the Shire was defended by a group of volunteers called "bounders" who minded its borders. Unbeknownst to the hobbits, the Shire was also guarded by the Dúnedain, the Rangers.

We can draw a couple of lessons from these arrangements. First, it is important to surround ourselves with people who have our best interests at heart and will help defend or protect us when needed. Second, it's important to build up certain boundaries in our own lives.

In the idyllic example of the Shire, the Rangers worked tirelessly to safeguard the hobbits, but there is no such exterior force for us that will defend our interior lives. That task falls to us entirely. At the end of the day, we have a duty to ourselves to establish boundaries that will protect our own mental, spiritual, emotional, and physical well-being. These boundaries can look like removing yourself from unhealthy relationships or environments, limiting your screentime or news intake, unsubscribing from certain newsletters or social media accounts, and otherwise being mindful of what you allow to influence your mind and heart. In doing so, we make room for the things that encourage us to thrive.

The Little Way of Thérèse of Lisieux

As I've contemplated what it means to be a hobbit at heart over the years, the spirituality of St. Thérèse of Lisieux has stayed with me. Her life was a lesson in smallness, surrender, and great love. In her autobiography, *The Story of a Soul,* St. Thérèse recounts the journey of her life as guided by a spirituality she called her "Little Way." It was a way that places an emphasis on humility, smallness, and complete trust in Jesus. As Thérèse put it in *The Story of a Soul*, the Little Way was "the way of spiritual childhood, the way of trust and absolute surrender."

St. Thérèse, often referred to as the Little Flower, was born in Alençon, France, in 1873. Much like John Ronald, Thérèse suffered the loss of her mother at a young age: Thérèse was only four years old when her mother passed away from breast cancer. As the youngest child of her family, Thérèse was sustained by the love of her father and older sisters but continued to suffer immensely for the rest of her life.

Driven by a fierce desire to give herself completely to Jesus, Thérèse ultimately entered the Carmelite convent in Lisieux where she took the religious name Sister Thérèse of the Child Jesus and the Holy Face. She lived a cloistered life of simplicity and obscurity until her death at age twenty-four in 1897.

At the request of her prioress and older sisters, Thérèse had written several manuscripts detailing her spiritual life. These were compiled into one spiritual memoir and published a year after her death. Her story and spiritual charism were immediately well received, and devotion to her Little Way grew. Despite her hidden and outwardly unremarkable life, St. Thérèse has since become one of the most popular saints in the world. She was canonized only twenty-eight years after her death and declared a Doctor of the Church in 1997, the youngest person to receive this recognition and one of only four women so named.

Considered the patroness of missions despite never leaving her convent, St. Thérèse and her Little Way teaches us that we do not have to wield great power or influence in order to make a difference. *The Story of a Soul* was published in 1898, when John Ronald was just six years old. At the time of her canonization, he was in his early thirties. While there is no proof that Tolkien ever read or directly drew inspiration from the writings of St. Thérèse, the hobbits have much in common with her emphasis on smallness, humility, and surrender.

The Hands of the Small

Nearly all of Tolkien's heroes, though they may span the ages and races of Middle-earth, have one thing in common: smallness. It is a theme foundational to *The Lord of the Rings*, one that is repeated often throughout Tolkien's Legendarium. While these heroes are most commonly small in the eyes of society, Tolkien emphasizes this smallness in the physically small stature of his hobbits. Their height ranges between two and four feet, and they would appear as children to men (such as when Pippin is mistaken for a child among the men of Gondor). Their histories are largely unknown to the "big folk" of Middle-earth; their way of life is simple and unassuming, perhaps even a little bit boring from our perspective. But it is in this simplicity that the most unlikely heroes are made.

And so, as Fate would have it, into the hands of these ordinary hobbits fell the most powerful device of the enemy, the One Ring. What followed should have been catastrophe, and yet Tolkien took his story in a different direction: Hope was found in folly, and victory was achieved in defeat.

At the Council of Elrond, doom lingered just over the horizon as representatives from every race of Middle-earth joined together to decide the fate of the One Ring. They discussed its history and power and the necessity of its destruction. Gandalf and Elrond explained that Sauron's pride had blinded him to the possibility that any who hold the One Ring would seek to destroy it, and so in taking this unprecedented path they would use their own perceived folly as a cloak. To the astonishment of all present at the council, it was the young Frodo Baggins who accepted the burden of bearing the One Ring to its destruction.

This tale was upheld by the most unexpected protagonists: It was not the elves in their immortal wisdom or men in their strength and courage who would carry the fate of Middle-earth, but hobbits in their meekness. Elrond spoke to those present at the Council:

> The road must be trod, but it will be very hard. And neither strength nor wisdom will carry us far upon it. This quest may be attempted by the weak with as much hope as the strong. Yet such is oft the course of deeds that move the wheels of the world: small hands do them because they must, while the eyes of the great are elsewhere. (*LOTR*, Book II, ch. 2)

While the wealthy and influential often seem to wield the most power in the world, Elrond reminds us that it is the small and humble who would bring about great change.

The Most Unlikely Heroes

In *The Hobbit*, Bilbo Baggins found himself in the midst of the most unlikely adventure a hobbit could go on. Deep within the tunnels of the Misty Mountains, he stumbled upon a small, golden ring—by accident, as he would think. Bilbo would soon learn that this was no ordinary ring, and it would be used to his benefit time and time again over the course of sixty years. While Bilbo's role within *The Lord of the Rings* diminished as the Ring passed to Frodo, it was at this moment that Bilbo's strength of will was highlighted. For all of its history, the One Ring had never been given up willingly—until Bilbo. The hobbit showed incredible strength in doing something that even someone as valiant as Isildur could not.

Frodo was the next bearer of the Ring. Despite feeling unworthy or unprepared to carry this burden, he accepted the task of carrying it toward its destruction. Because of his humility, firm sense of duty, and love for the Shire, Frodo was able to withstand the power of the Ring for far longer than someone with more pride or ambition.

Sam Gamgee, too, carried the Ring for a time. After Frodo was stung by the spider Shelob, Sam mistakenly believed that Frodo had been killed. Understanding the weight of Frodo's task, he took the Ring upon himself and resolved to finish Frodo's quest alone. The Ring tempted him, but it was ultimately his love for Frodo and his "plain hobbit-sense" that allowed him to refuse its call. He understood "in the core of his heart that he was not large enough to bear such a burden" (*LOTR*, Book VI, ch. 1). Sam understood that to wield a power as great as the Ring would be a burden, one he ultimately did not desire.

Smallness is often considered a disadvantage, something Tolkien subverted and used to the hobbits' advantage. After the Battle of the Pelennor Fields, Merry remarked that it was "not always a misfortune being overlooked" (*LOTR*, Book V, ch. 8). Frodo and Sam were able to sneak into Mordor because of their smallness; had Aragorn led an army behind them, they would have immediately been perceived by

Sauron. (If you have been wondering why the eagles couldn't have simply flown the Ring to Mount Doom, this is one of the reasons.) Both their physical stature and hidden life led hobbits to be severely underestimated, to the detriment of their enemies.

Becoming spiritually "small" does not mean becoming a doormat, becoming physically small, being quiet, or being unnecessarily passive. Being small does not mean making oneself vulnerable to abuse or injustice. Instead, it is like being whittled down until only the strong core remains. Smallness means being willing to travel light, to set aside whatever may be unneeded or hinders your purpose, and to rely on a deeper source of strength. This kind of strength in humility is the work of a lifetime.

While hobbits were the primary protagonists of *The Lord of the Rings* and the plainest examples of Tolkien's preference for small heroes, we will also meet several other characters along our journey who exemplify this theme of spiritual or cultural smallness.

Éowyn, the Lady of Rohan, had been raised in a culture that valued valor in battle above all things. And to her great disappointment, she was commanded to remain behind in Meduseld rather than ride out to war with her kindred. After disguising herself as a male soldier called Dernhelm and riding out to battle, Éowyn found herself standing before the dreaded Witch-king of Angmar. It had been prophesied that no man would be able to kill him, but she confounded him by revealing that she was not a man but a woman. In her defeat of the Witch-king, her perceived weakness was her strength.

Despite being the rightful heir of Isildur, Aragorn presented himself as the rugged outcast Strider. He humbled himself, enduring the scorn and suspicion of all he met for many years. Even as the War of the Ring drew to a close, Aragorn waited to come into his kingdom until Sauron had been utterly defeated. His patience and careful discernment throughout *The Lord of the Rings* should serve as a model for all those who wish to lead.

Similarly, Gandalf was one of the most powerful beings in Middle-earth and yet refused dominion or leadership over any realm or people. He offered counsel without coercion, guidance without domination. Despite his power and importance, Gandalf sacrificed himself while fighting against the Balrog of Moria in order to allow the rest of the Fellowship to flee to safety.

All of these characters reflect the sense of smallness described in St. Thérèse's Little Way. The hero sees their path illuminated by the light of humility and duty, while the enemy is blinded by the shadow of his own pride. The hero is carried by the arms of Providence toward goodness, while the enemy relentlessly pursues control and domination to his own demise. Within each of Tolkien's small heroes, we can catch glimpses of the person we were meant to become. In reading Tolkien, we can learn to become as trusting as Bilbo, as steadfast as Frodo, as anchored as Samwise, as undaunted as Éowyn, as patient as Aragorn, and more.

Frodo began his quest in complete humility, "acknowledging that he was wholly inadequate to the task" (*Letters*, 246). He did so out of love, compelled by his desire to save Middle-earth from destruction regardless of what it might cost him.

In the end, against all odds, the Ring was unmade, and Sauron was defeated by a fellowship rooted in humility, love, and surrender. Tolkien's heroes were the ones who ultimately succeeded by simply plodding on despite all odds or the loss of hope. Weighed down by despair and yet not fully drowned, they trudged toward the light with their last ounce of strength and will. And in the end, it was enough. This is the "little way of the halfling."

THE ROAD GOES ON

In what ways do you feel "small"? How can this smallness be used to your advantage? Reflect on the ways that you have seen strength in simplicity. Are there other people in your life who embody this dynamic? What do you admire about them? How might you take additional steps to become little so that you might become more free?

Chapter 4

Find Your Fellowship

Values: Fellowship, Respect, Community, and Devotion

> You can trust us to stick to you through thick and thin—to the bitter end. And you can trust us to keep any secret of yours—closer than you keep it yourself. But you cannot trust us to let you face trouble alone, and go off without a word. We are your friends, Frodo.
>
> *LOTR*, Book I, ch. 5

After being pursued by mysterious Black Riders, Frodo has finally arrived safely at his new home in Crickhollow. Though far less grand than Bag End, it would be a perfectly lovely place to call home. If only he could truly stay here, he wishes. Instead, he knows that his next steps will lead him out of the Shire altogether. And he knows he must go alone. What he doesn't know is that his friends have secretly unraveled all of his plans and decided they're going with him. Frodo is alarmed by the realization that he hadn't kept his secret as well as he had hoped, and he laments that he feels he can't trust anyone. Sam's response emphasizes the core of friendship as something built on mutual trust, devotion, and love.

The most poignant theme of *The Lord of the Rings* is that of fellowship—the first volume's title is *The Fellowship of the Ring,* which is the chosen name for the nine companions who will carry the Ring to its destruction. Friendship is essential to a fulfilling life. It comes in many forms, but it doesn't necessarily come easily. It requires effort from all parties involved, along with mutual respect and trust. Tolkien teaches us that we can't and shouldn't go on the journeys of life alone. In this chapter, we will examine the different kinds of friendships seen in *The Lord of the Rings*.

Since my early twenties, I've moved more than a dozen times. From Phoenix to Tucson to the Caribbean to Michigan, Florida, England, California, and Indiana, I've had to rebuild my community all over again each and every time. More than anything, I've learned that finding community requires consistent effort and proactivity. Waiting for people to show up and put in all the work will almost always leave you feeling lonely and resentful. If you want to make a friend, first *be* a friend.

Ask yourself what qualities in friendship are important to you and then strive to embody those qualities for someone else. If you wish you were invited to more parties, start by hosting events of your own. If you hoped your community would have set up a meal train when you had a baby, organize one for another new parent. Introduce yourself to people, invite people out to coffee, and take a sincere interest in their lives.

In our digital age, most people don't know how to be proactive in making new friends or nourishing their existing friendships. I understand that it can be frightening to reach out for connection. It's uncomfortable, vulnerable, time-consuming, sometimes embarrassing—and it might make you late for dinner. But as Tolkien's stories show, it is worth it. It won't always work out—your values and personality will not be compatible with everyone—and that's okay. As time passes and you stay consistent in your efforts, new friendships will begin to take root and blossom.

I have also learned from Tolkien that there are many different kinds of friendships, and there is room in life for all of them. You will have friends who annoy you from time to time, like Pippin does for Gandalf. You will have friends who challenge your perspective, like Gimli does for Legolas. Like Sam carrying Frodo, there will be times in life where you will need to carry friends through difficult seasons—and in other times, you will need them to carry *you*. Nurturing these relationships creates a network of support for when life gets hard, and we all need one another.

Over the course of his quest, Frodo's friendship with Sam Gamgee would prove lifesaving. He quite literally would not have made it out of the story alive without him. Sam's love for Frodo was rooted in a deep sense of duty, and Frodo's respect for Sam grew abundantly over the course of their journey. Sam recognized Frodo's need and made great sacrifices to help carry him—literally and figuratively, at times—through his journey. And though Frodo was at first uncomfortable accepting his help, doing so honored the bond of their friendship and increased his trust in Sam.

Their relationship was inspired by Tolkien's experience during the First World War with military officers and their batmen (*Letters*, 187). The role of the batman was to care for the material needs of his superior, managing practical or smaller tasks in order to allow the officer to rest, plan, or instruct other soldiers. Tolkien deeply admired these batmen, writing that he regarded them as far superior to himself despite the fact that he outranked them.

When departing from Crickhollow, Merry, Pippin, and Sam committed to going forward with Frodo, while Fredegar Bolger intended to remain behind. While some might judge Fredegar harshly for being unwilling to leave, staying behind was also done at a great peril. And it's not as if he had no part to play. He later sounded the alarm when the Black Riders broke into the Crickhollow home, scaring them off. Fredegar Bolger can serve as a reminder that you don't have to follow all of your friends into Mordor in order to support them. He set his own boundaries, which other hobbits respected, and did as much as he could.

The friendship of Merry and Pippin was rooted in their shared experience; they had grown up together in the Shire and had grown very close along the way. They were, in many ways, an archetype of best friends. Always looking out for one another, the two were on equal terms and knew each other well. Their separation on the plains of Rohan was a painful one, and their reunion in Minas Tirith was joyous.

The friendships between the hobbits made up the core of the Fellowship of the Ring, carrying the love of the Shire out into the wild wide world. As Frodo, Sam, Merry, and Pippin were each called onto different paths along their way, their commitment to one another brought them back together in the end.

The Fellowship of the Ring

The Fellowship of the Ring was comprised of representatives from each race of Middle-earth, bringing the hobbits together with an elf, a dwarf, a wizard, and two humans. Despite their differences, they were united with one common purpose that overruled their own personal comforts or desires.

While the hobbits were the central focus of the story in many ways, the Ring concerned all the peoples of Middle-earth. The Fellowship of the Ring was assembled to reflect the shared responsibility of every race to resist Sauron. As the Fellowship of the Ring departed from Rivendell, the fate of the world would rest on the shoulders of four halflings, two men, an elf, a dwarf, and a wizard. These nine companions are chosen to combat the nine Black Riders, the Nazgûl, servants of Sauron intent on returning the One Ring to their master.

Although elves and dwarves have been at odds for centuries, Legolas and Gimli formed a fast friendship on their journey. As the Fellowship came to the West-door of Moria, Gandalf explained that this passageway had been made in the Second Age chiefly for the use of the elves. "Those were happier days, when there was still close friendship at times between the folk of different race, even between dwarves and elves," he says (*LOTR*, Book II, ch. 4).

The dwarvish doors into Moria were marked with the phrase, "Speak, friend, and enter," and would not open until the elvish word for friend was spoken (*LOTR*, Book II, ch. 4). The ancient friendship between the two races had long been broken, however, and the road lay in ruin. The friendship between Legolas and Gimli represented a healing of the rift between these two peoples. It was also reminiscent of the friendship between the elven-smith Celebrimbor and the dwarven-smith Narvi, who together crafted the Doors of Durin. Even after the War of the Ring ended and the quest of the Fellowship was completed, Legolas and Gimli remained close friends. It is told in appendix A of *The Lord of the Rings* that after the death of Aragorn, both Legolas and Gimli would leave Middle-earth and come to the Blessed Realm. As a testament to their bond, Gimli was the only dwarf in all of Tolkien's tales who would take this journey.

Within the Fellowship, Gandalf served primarily as a counselor and guide. As each new path needed to be discerned, he did not force his will on the others but allowed Frodo to choose freely. He was also an exemplar of heroic duty and sacrifice; Gandalf understood that the task of carrying the Ring was appointed to Frodo and so prioritized Frodo's safety over his own.

After the Council of Elrond, Boromir's path was meant to lead him back to Minas Tirith. Boromir was a noble and proud man who had valiantly defended Gondor all of his life, and all of the information revealed at the Council of Elrond came as strange and new to him. He had grown up in the shadow of Mordor and without the counsel of the elves and their histories. Because of this, his understanding of Sauron was based only on the destruction he had seen firsthand. His relationship with the other members of the Fellowship was strained at times, but his participation in the company was invaluable. Ultimately, after Boromir fell to the temptation of the Ring and tried to take it from Frodo, he realized his error and spent the final hours of his life defending the lives of those most vulnerable.

Aragorn's farewell to Boromir was telling of their friendship. When Aragorn found him, Boromir confessed that he tried to take the Ring from Frodo. Rather than admonish him, Aragorn assured him that he had achieved a great victory by defending the hobbits so valiantly. Aragorn also assured him that Minas Tirith would not fall, comforting Boromir as he breathed his last breath. Even after Boromir's death, Aragorn did not reveal his fault to Legolas and

Gimli until much later. Instead, he preserved the memory of Boromir as a hero. In these final moments, Aragorn acted as a friend and counselor to Boromir and promised that his sacrifice was not in vain.

None Should Walk Alone

In contrast to the close bond of the Fellowship of the Ring, many of Tolkien's most tragic characters had something in common: an intentional withdrawal from community. As a rule, evil is able to work more effectively when we are isolated and withdrawn from our own "fellowships." While it is not always unhealthy to be alone, the deliberate isolation of the self can be detrimental.

We see the dangers of isolation in the origins of Sauron. In the beginning of Tolkien's world, Morgoth sought out power and glory on his own terms apart from Ilúvatar's designs, wandering alone and isolating himself until he became "a liar without shame" or mercy (*Silm*, Valaquenta). According to Tolkien lore, as Morgoth's power grew, a Maia called Mairon was seduced into his service (see *Parma Eldalamberon 17*, 183). Mairon separated himself from the rest of the Ainur, following Morgoth in pursuit of the power to shape and order the world according to his own plans. Ultimately, Mairon became the greatest of Morgoth's servants: He was known by many names, but the elves called him Sauron. After Morgoth's defeat, he was given the chance to return to the Blessed Realm for judgment but instead fled and once again isolated himself. Without counsel or guidance, Sauron chose a return to the ways of Morgoth and ultimately followed him down the same ruinous path.

Similarly, when the elven-smith Fëanor made the blessed gems called Silmarils, he grew to love them with a "greedy love" and hid them from all others (*Silm*, ch. 7). Like Sauron, Fëanor was also targeted by Morgoth; in isolating himself from the noise of all other elves, he heard the whispers of Morgoth more clearly. Ultimately, Fëanor's single-minded pursuit of vengeance would bring about his own death: He rushed ahead of his kindred toward Morgoth, where he found himself surrounded by Balrogs and "with few friends about him" and perished soon after (*Silm*, ch. 13).

Even before the Ring came to him, Sméagol had a tendency to wander off alone. He loved to tunnel and dig, always in pursuit of roots and beginnings and secrets. This natural inclination was only amplified by the power of the Ring, which Sméagol used for wicked purposes until he found himself alone and friendless. He wandered across the wilderness until he eventually hid himself deep within the Misty Mountains.

As the Third Age waned on and the Ring still remained hidden, the wizard Saruman slowly distanced himself from his peers. In secret, he had grown to desire the One Ring for himself and begun to seek it out. In his isolation, he nurtured his pride until he began to believe that he himself could supplant Sauron, using his own devices against him. Without the guidance of the other wizards or the elves, Saruman fell to the evil he initially sought to defeat. This theme of the dangers of isolation recurs often in Tolkien's works, echoing down the long ages of the history of Tolkien's story world.

Isolation leaves a person susceptible to the seduction of evil, whereas community acts as a shield. Where there is community, there is accountability, security, and understanding. A good friend will know you well enough to notice when you're straying from your purpose; they will call you out when you betray your own values. A good friend will accompany you through your suffering, help you back up when you fall, carry you when you are weak, and remind you who you are and where your home is.

St. John the Evangelist

Tolkien had a special devotion to St. John the Evangelist, whom he referred to as his patron saint (*Letters*, 308). Not only is St. John the patron saint of authors, but he is also considered the patron saint of friendship. According to Christian tradition, John was among the closest disciples and friends of Jesus. He is referred to throughout the Gospel of John as "the disciple whom Jesus loved" (John 13:23;

19:26; 20:2) and was one of the few witnesses to Christ's Transfiguration. He remained at the foot of the Cross during the Crucifixion, where he was entrusted with the care of Jesus's mother, Mary (John 19:27). When all other apostles fled, John alone remained alongside the women at the foot of the Cross. St. John's dedication to Christ as both friend and Lord can serve as a powerful inspiration for Christians, prompting us to love those around us more fully even when it comes with a personal cost.

Tolkien's Life of Fellowship

For the young John Ronald, friendship wasn't something that merely enriched or brought additional positivity to life—it was necessary for survival. As an orphan who was also largely estranged from his remaining biological family, friendship would take on a whole new value that would see him through some of the most difficult years of his life.

In his teen years, John Ronald was a part of a small clique dubbed the Tea Club and Barrovian Society, or TCBS. The TCBS had begun with regular meetings in the library office and in Barrow Stores while its members were students at King Edward's School in Birmingham and continued wherever possible after the boys had matriculated.

This group had varied participation over the years, but its core members were Geoffrey Bache Smith, Christopher Wiseman, Robert Gilson, and J. R. R. Tolkien. They shared a common goal of making a lasting impact on the world through art and writing. These friendships would become more important than any of these young men could have imagined as the world would soon descend into the chaos of World War I. As each of them enlisted and was ultimately sent to war, they would continue writing to one another about their experiences of battle and life on the front lines.

Out of the four core members of the TCBS, only two would survive the First World War; both Smith and Gilson were killed during the Battle of the Somme. Their deaths compounded the horrors of war and profoundly affected Tolkien. After the war, Tolkien would name his firstborn son after Christopher Wiseman. Although the TCBS would not last forever, it would remain in Tolkien's heart, setting the foundation for a life grounded in intentional friendship.

In the years that followed, Tolkien would form close connections with many other friend groups and organizations. While living and working at Oxford, Tolkien was an active member in a like-minded group known as the Inklings. Though membership changed over the years, its most influential members included C. S. Lewis, Owen Barfield, Charles Williams, Hugo Dyson, and J. R. R. Tolkien. They typically met on Tuesday afternoons at various Oxford pubs, most notably The Eagle and Child or The Lamb and Flag, where they would read aloud and critique each other's written work.

While they did not follow any formal rules or bylaws, the Inklings gathered for the common purpose of encouraging each other in their literary work. Throughout Tolkien's letters, he often refers to conversations and meetings with various members of the Inklings. They invested in one another and shared their lives with each other. It is clear from these examples that he placed a high importance on maintaining a social life; these friendships were not born simply out of convenience or as a way to pass the time—they were deliberate and purposeful.

J. R. R. Tolkien's *Lord of the Rings* and C. S. Lewis's *Chronicles of Narnia* are two of the world's best-selling stories, and I believe the authors' literary fellowship and literary success went hand-in-hand. We were made for fellowship, and the legacy of the friendship of these two literary giants serves as a bright reminder that in supporting one another, we can accomplish great things.

THE ROAD GOES ON

After looking at the friendships in both Tolkien's life and works, what stands out to you? In what ways is your social life strong—how has it supported you? What else are you looking for in friendship? Examine what you need from friendship and strive to offer or embody that same thing for someone else.

Chapter 5

STEWARD THE "FIELDS THAT YOU KNOW"

Values: Leadership, Stewardship, Discernment, and Justice

> Take off your golden ring! Your hand's more fair without it. Come back! Leave your game and sit down beside me! We must talk a while more, and think about the morning. Tom must teach the right road, and keep your feet from wandering.
>
> *LOTR*, Book I, ch. 7

After saying goodbye to Frodo's home in Crickhollow, the hobbits are soon after lost within the Old Forest. And to make matters worse, they seem to have angered an apparently sentient willow tree. Frodo calls for help instinctively, without knowing whom he hopes will answer. And then into our story strolls a creature even older than the Ents, one who remembers the first raindrop. Iarwain Ben-adar he is called, oldest and fatherless—he is Tom Bombadil. He wears yellow boots, a bright blue coat, and a tall hat with a blue feather; in his hands, he carries white water lilies. His melodic voice assuages the wrath of Old Man Willow and bids the four bewildered hobbits to follow him, guiding them through the Old Forest and toward the refuge of his home.

There, deep in the forest, dwelt Tom Bombadil with Goldberry in safety and in bliss. His presence was astonishing and enigmatic; he was ancient and powerful and completely unaffected by Sauron's Ring. When asked who Tom was, Goldberry simply responded, "He is, as you have seen him. . . . He is the master of wood, water, and hill" (*LOTR*, Book I, ch. 7). But the land did not belong to Tom—all living things belonged to themselves. Tom Bombadil was completely free of any desire to dominate or rule. His very existence seemed to mock Sauron. Tom was the embodiment of self-mastery; he was master of himself.

The lessons to be learned from Tom Bombadil are manifold. He laughed in the presence of Sauron's most dreadful weapon. He confidently used the power of his voice to liberate the hobbits—not once, but twice. Tom Bombadil teaches us that all living things have their own worth and dignity.

Like Tom Bombadil, each of us has been entrusted with some measure of authority. How we use this authority is important; our voices have power and our actions are consequential. More than anything, we must care without self-interest for the things placed in our authority. In contrast to Tom Bombadil, Sauron saw all living things as tools for his own use and domination. He disregarded the inherent dignity and value of other living things, using them only as a means to an end. To reject Sauron was to reject the temptation of domination. The world does not belong to you, but you have been entrusted with the span of your life within it. As we learn from Tom Bombadil, along with Tolkien's other stewards and leaders, we can learn how to become masters of ourselves.

Rejecting Domination

In pursuit of peace and order, Sauron was willing to enslave the peoples of Middle-earth by force or by manipulation. The antidote to Sauron's tyranny was stewardship, or guardianship. Through acknowledging that they were not meant to be the supreme ruler or wield universal authority, Tolkien's heroes defended goodness without falling into the methods of the enemy. In the same way that Tom Bombadil was a master and yet did not claim ownership of his land or its inhabitants, a good leader recognizes whatever authority has been given to them without claiming mastery over it unequivocally.

One example of such a steward is Faramir, son of Denethor and brother of Boromir. Unlike his brother, Faramir did not seek out glory or renown. Whereas Boromir was tempted and ultimately tried to take the Ring from Frodo, Faramir had the same opportunity to claim the Ring for himself and made no attempt. He was truly pure of heart, explaining that he did not love strength for its own sake but only for its use in defending the good, the true, and the beautiful. In a conversation with Frodo on battle and war he said, "I do not love the bright sword for its sharpness, nor the arrow for its swiftness, nor the warrior for his glory. I love only that which they defend" (*LOTR*, Book IV, ch. 5). In this, Faramir and Frodo were aligned in their love for their homeland and its inhabitants; both were willing to leave them behind in hopes of defending them.

Gandalf was also a steward. He did not wish for mastery of any people or realm. He understood that his task was simply to help those who would resist Sauron. His allegiance was not to any one ruler or land but to all of Middle-earth. He said to Denethor, "But all worthy things that are in peril as the world now stands, those are my care. And for my part, I shall not wholly fail of my task, though Gondor should perish, if anything passes through this night that can still grow fair or bear fruit and flower again in days to come. For I also am a steward. Did you not know?" (*LOTR*, Book V, ch. 1). If all other realms fell to Sauron, but one small hillside remained free, then he would not have failed in his task. Unlike Saruman who took up residence and authority of Isengard, Gandalf roamed from realm to realm without any home of his own. In this, he is reminiscent of Christ, who spent most of his ministry traveling and said, "The Son of Man has nowhere to lay his head" (Matthew 8:20).

Stewardship of the Earth

We all have a duty to be careful stewards of our common home, the earth. For Christians, these instructions are given directly from God in the account of creation detailed in Genesis. As industrialization and overconsumption continue to ravage the planet, this command should remain at the front of our minds.

In the summer of 1955, Tolkien traveled to Italy with his daughter Priscilla. He wrote that they went together to Assisi in early August, attending a Mass for the feast of St. Clare of Assisi (*Letters*, 167). Sts. Francis and Clare of Assisi both placed an emphasis on care for the environment as a part of their Christian life and ministry. Tolkien may have resonated with their spirituality, as he consistently showed a love for the natural world (especially trees). Many of his works emphasize the beauty, power, and dignity of the natural, created world and in turn oppose industrialization. Tolkien's heroes were those who cooperated with the natural order and natural world; his villains are those who sought to manipulate, dominate, or destroy it.

Ents, especially, can be seen as advocates for the natural world. Detailed in *The Silmarillion*, the creation of the Ents was a response to the coming of men and dwarves who would threaten plant life. They were made as spirits who bore the likeness of trees and would advocate for all things that had roots. In the War of the Ring, they were prompted to action by Saruman's ravaging of their forests. Together with Merry and Pippin, they marched upon Isengard, flooding the area and confining Saruman to his tower. They represented Tolkien's love and care for the environment, presenting an image of the natural world defending itself. Because such creatures do not exist in our own primary reality, the responsibility falls onto our human shoulders to advocate for the earth.

The Lord of the Rings has deeply influenced the way I view the natural world. In seeing the trees spring to life and defend themselves in Middle-earth, I have begun to better understand my own connection and duty to the natural world. Because of Tolkien, I appreciate the flowers in bloom or the leaves as they change colors more than I did before. I understand more keenly my own duty to care for the earth, and this conviction has inspired me to try to live more sustainably, reducing waste and making my daily decisions with future generations in mind. I have also learned to prioritize time spent outdoors and offline, discovering a profound peace in refocusing my attention to the cares in my immediate sphere of influence.

Treebeard described Saruman as having a "mind of metal and wheels." Like Sauron, Saruman saw living things as nothing more than a means to an end (*LOTR*, Book III, ch. 4). As someone who has turned away from his purpose in pursuit of power and dominion, Saruman represents the antithesis of who I want to be. Instead, Treebeard's wisdom can prompt us to reject frivolous uses of technology that deplete natural resources (such as generative AI), respect the purpose and worth of all living things, and be faithful stewards of our own communities.

The Time Given to You

We are also stewards of time. Each of us has been born into this specific point in time for a reason. Frodo lamented to Gandalf that he wished the Ring had not come to him, and Gandalf's reply speaks to the heart of this feeling: "So do all who live to see such times. But that is not for them to decide. All we have to decide is what to do with the time that is given us" (*LOTR*, Book I, ch. 2). Gandalf later restates the same sentiment before the Men of the West as they prepare to march upon Sauron: While we cannot control what may happen after our time has ended, we have a moral duty to uproot "the evil in the fields that we know, so that those who live after may have clean earth to till. What weather they shall have is not ours to rule" (*LOTR*, Book V, ch. 9).

In ages past, the average person was largely unaware of events unfolding across the world. Instead, their care and advocacy would have been devoted to their own local communities. Advances in technology and the advent of social media have made us more connected than we ever have been. These tools have brought awareness of injustices happening in every part of the world, opening our eyes to all the work that must be done. This is a good thing! However, the weight of this knowledge can also be a source of great anxiety—I know it is for me. Our minds and hearts were not made to bear the weight of the entire world's suffering. It can feel impossible to reconcile the reality of our duty to one another with the knowledge that we cannot solve all the world's problems. Like Denethor with the Palantir, we might find ourselves losing hope when faced with the horrors of war, corruption, and disaster across the world; sometimes, it may feel as if Sauron has already won.

In these moments, I turn to prayer, asking for the intercession of our Blessed Mother for the sake of all her children throughout the world. But then, I also turn to places in which I can have an impact, beginning in my own communities and then branching out farther whenever possible. You may not be able to help someone on the other side of the globe today, but there are people in your own neighborhood for whom your help can make a lasting difference. It is good to be informed, but do not let the never-resting news cycle paralyze you with fear or anxiety. Instead, let the things you are reading, hearing, and watching online prompt you to action. You were born into this time for a purpose, and you have a duty to uproot evil in the "fields that you know." Our impact may seem small, but like each member of the Fellowship, we can work toward our common goal one step at a time.

Sauron's False Peace

Ultimately, Sauron offered a false peace. His promises were empty—nothing more than a mirage or distorted reflection in the water. His goal was to create a world where his control was absolute. All would be subservient to him; with the Rings of Power, he would control their very minds, bending them toward whatever his goals might be.

Tolkien wrote that Sauron hated "wasteful friction" (*Morgoth's Ring*, 394), preferring a false peace void of any conflict. By contrast, true peace will always result in friction. To be a peacemaker requires rooting out injustice, not just pacification or compliance. To oppose injustice is to dismantle oppressive systems or hierarchies; the pursuit of justice is naturally disruptive. It might even make you late for dinner. But all Christians are called to this work, as emphasized in the Beatitudes: "Blessed are the peacemakers, for they will be called children of God" (Matthew 5:9).

When Théoden was tempted by Saruman with an offer of peace, the offer was ultimately rejected because the king knew that true peace was only possible where justice prevailed. As Théoden stated, true peace requires taking risks and opposing injustice. To Saruman, he proclaimed, "We will have peace, when you and all your works have perished—and the works of your dark master to whom you would deliver us. You are a liar, Saruman, and a corrupter of men's hearts" (*LOTR*, Book III, ch. 10).

Inspired by the examples of Tolkien's noble characters like Tom Bombadil, Gandalf, Faramir, Aragorn, and Théoden, we can work toward peace in our own hearts and communities. We are each stewards of our lives, time, relationships, communities, and the earth. It is imperative for each of us to acknowledge, respect, and fight for the dignity of all people. In doing so, we can each begin to move the wheels of the world toward a true and lasting peace.

THE ROAD GOES ON

Reflect on your role as a steward: You are a steward of time, the people in your care (for example, students, children, or employees), the earth and its resources, and your own gifts and talents. How can you become a better steward to all for which you are responsible? Consider writing down three things you can take action on this week. For longer-term concerns, begin by creating a vision board.

Chapter 6

WELCOME THE WANDERER

Values: Generosity, Availability, Connection, and Hospitality

> And so at last they all came to the Last Homely House, and found its doors flung wide. . . . His house was perfect, whether you liked food, or sleep, or work, or story-telling, or singing, or just sitting and thinking best, or a pleasant mixture of them all. Evil things did not come into that valley.
>
> *The Hobbit*, ch. 3

Frodo's eyes open to an unfamiliar, yet not unwelcome, sight. After being pierced by a Morgul-blade and pursued by Black Riders, he had been in grave danger, but all appears well now. Frodo is safe in the house of Elrond Half-elven. Here, many have gathered for the Council of Elrond to decide the fate of the One Ring. The home of Elrond is a balm to a weary soul and a safe haven for the hunted. Through his willingness to open his home, to become a diplomat and coordinator of community, Elrond will play a crucial role in the downfall of Sauron.

If we truly believe that we belong to one another, being welcoming to those in need is an easily recognized duty. Throughout his entire journey, Frodo's quest was safeguarded by friends along the way. The most important or defining of these was in the home of Elrond in Rivendell. There, Frodo's quest was fully realized, and he was officially sent forth. We have examined how to respond when Fate calls us away from home, but now we will explore the ways that we might be asked to welcome someone else into our own lives.

One of the defining traits of hobbits is a fondness for visitors. They kept their cupboards stocked and their schedules consistent. When Bilbo bid farewell to the dwarves at the end of his journey in *The Hobbit*, he offered a standing invitation for tea: "If ever you are passing my way, don't wait to knock! Tea is at four; but any of you are welcome at any time!" (*The Hobbit*, ch. 18). While they were known for their hospitality, both Bilbo and Frodo would learn on their adventures what it meant to be on the receiving end of hospitality. Each journey was punctuated with different examples of the peoples of Middle-earth opening their homes to these hobbits. In the end, their willingness to be welcoming proved essential. Neither Bilbo nor Frodo would have survived without the willingness of both friends and strangers to be a safe haven in their time of need.

Half-Elven Hospitality

Because Elrond was a descendant of both elf and human, he brought a unique perspective to his care for the peoples of Middle-earth. Elrond's home was practical and communal yet still maintained the otherworldly atmosphere of the elves. In Rivendell, his visitors' clothing was mended, their physical and mental health was refreshed, their plans were improved, and they were equipped for the road ahead. Everyone who came to Rivendell left better off than when they came.

Rivendell was originally established in the middle of the Second Age, after the fall of the elven realm of Eregion. As the power of Sauron grew and the elves began to diminish, Rivendell became one of the last strongholds to stand against Sauron. In addition to safeguarding elves, Elrond also fostered the heirs of Isildur in their youth. There, they were kept hidden and safe from those who sought to end the line of kings. Protected by one of the three elven Rings, Rivendell survived all the way through the Third Age when Fate would bring a handful of hobbits to Elrond's doorstep. Inspired by his example, we can draw on our unique gifts and circumstances to become a safe haven for others.

Finding Safe Haven in Middle-earth

In *The Hobbit*, Bilbo and the dwarves would have been utterly lost if Elrond had not extended his hospitality and advice to their company. Even after leaving Rivendell, they would be rescued by eagles, guided and protected by Beorn, and aided by many of the men from Laketown. If any of these gracious hosts had turned our traveling company away, the course of their entire story would've been changed—for the worse, indeed.

Frodo's journey was similarly sustained by points of refuge along the way. While being pursued by Black Riders on the way to Crickhollow, Frodo and his companions found a safe haven in the home of Farmer Maggot. Only a few chapters later, the hobbits would find themselves needing to be rescued, not once, but twice by Tom Bombadil.

Even as the road took them farther from home than they could have imagined, Frodo and Sam would be sustained by the care of others. In the brambles of Ithilien, Frodo and Sam were captured by Captain Faramir of Gondor. An unexpected grace, their meeting turned from peril to protection. Faramir offered them refreshment, a brief respite from unguarded sleep, advice, and even gifts upon their departure. As they bid Faramir farewell, Frodo recalled the words of Elrond, "It was said to me by Elrond Halfelven that I should find friendship upon the way, secret and unlooked for. Certainly I looked for no such friendship as you have shown. To have found it turns evil to great good" (*LOTR*, Book IV, ch. 7).

The hospitality of the good and kind folk of Middle-earth proved, time and time again, to be lifesaving. Frodo wouldn't have made it to Rivendell, let alone Mordor, without these refuges along the way. It was a refreshment for weary souls and a comfort that gave them the strength to continue along their hard journeys. Whether from a half-elven lord or the simplest of hobbits, these seemingly small acts of kindness made all the difference. If it weren't for the help of so many of Tolkien's characters along the way, the quest to destroy the Ring would have never succeeded. Recognizing this theme in *The Lord of the Rings* can prompt us to carry an intentional sense of hospitality into our own lives. Each of us can keep our eyes open for those who might need a safe haven, whether physically or emotionally.

Tolkien the Orphan

For the young Tolkien, the Christian duty to care for the widow and orphan was not an abstract concept. John Ronald suffered alongside his mother when she was widowed at a young age, and he understood the sacrifices she made to care for her sons without the help of her family. And when she died, he became keenly aware of how vulnerable it is to be an orphan; this experience formed his response to others in difficult situations.

One anecdote recalls Tolkien being struck by the piety of a homeless man to whom he offered alms, later remarking to the parish priest that the man "looked a great deal more like St. Joseph than the statue in the church—at any rate, St. Joseph on the way to Egypt" (*Letters*, 89). He recognized that we all have a duty to one another, but especially to those with great need. This obligation is one of the most emphasized teachings in the Bible, as noted in the book of James: "Religion that is pure and undefiled before God, the Father, is this: to care for orphans and widows in their distress, and to keep oneself unstained by the world" (James 1:27).

Benedictine Hospitality

This charism of welcome woven through the pages of *The Lord of the Rings* (and *The Hobbit*, of course) is reminiscent of Benedictine hospitality, a way of life named after St. Benedict of Nursia. Benedict was a gentle and disciplined monk and abbot who pioneered monastic life in fifth- and sixth-century Italy. He wrote a series of guidelines for monks to follow, which has come to be known as the Rule of St. Benedict. In 1964, when Tolkien was in his early seventies, Benedict was declared by Pope Paul VI to be the patron saint of Europe.

The Rule of St. Benedict outlines his guidelines for monastic life that have been widely applied to monasticism across the world, with many principles that can be adopted to the lay Christian life. Benedictines do not necessarily work outside of their monasteries but rather emphasize prayer, work, and hospitality toward guests who come to them.

Importantly, the Rule of St. Benedict states that all guests should be received as Christ; this teaching came directly from Christ himself when he said, "For I was hungry and you gave me food, I was thirsty and you gave me something to drink, I was a stranger and you welcomed me, I was naked and you gave me clothing, I was sick and you took care of me, I was in prison and you visited me" (Matthew 25:35–36). Christians practice a way of life that makes space for the unexpected—leaving room for the visitor, for the inconvenient, for the refugee, for the sick, for the poor. Making space for others is, in essence, making space for Christ. Through the lens of faith, caring for the poor, hungry, unhoused, sick, imprisoned, disabled, refugee, young, and elderly is a privileged place to meet the divine.

If we believe meaning and purpose are ultimately tied to love, we must take steps to put love into action, which means being willing to make sacrifices for the good of the other. These are not the kind of actions that depend on feelings. This kind of love is not something that you can fall in and out of, but rather something that you must choose every day.

Unglamorous Love

Tolkien never mentioned if there were dirty dishes in the sink at Tom Bombadil's house or floors that needed sweeping, or children who needed to be kept on schedules at Farmer Maggot's, or if they really even felt like having visitors at all in Rivendell. In the context of our own lives, those are important details, but they should come second to the command to love.

Sometimes, we may find it difficult to be welcoming or accommodating, but these are precisely the moments when we have the greatest opportunity to show love as we put aside our own fears or discomfort for the sake of others. The impact of practicing an openness to others cannot be overstated. Inviting friends over for a meal or drinks, being open to relatives dropping by for a visit, or making space for loved ones to stay over are wonderful ways to be hospitable. Everyone is in a different season of life, so practicing hospitality in a physical sense will look different for each of us.

There are certain habits that you can adopt if you would like to host people regularly. Keeping certain go-to foods stocked in your cupboards, dedicating an area for guests to stay—whether a guest bedroom or purchasing an air mattress—and keeping your home generally tidy are practical ways to begin. If you are new to hosting, you should start small by inviting one or two people over at a time. I have always enjoyed hosting and throwing parties and have consciously worked to make my home into a hub for gatherings. If your circumstances do not allow you to welcome people physically into your home, you can easily adopt this attitude of hospitality by meeting someone at the library, café, or park.

Preparing to welcome others is less about creating the perfect conditions for hospitality and more about taking small steps toward intentionally making room for others in your life. The truest value of hospitality isn't found in the food itself, the entertainment, or the effort expended to impress others with Pinterest-worthy homes. It is found in the way that we allow ourselves to love with an open heart. We need to make room in our hearts, our schedules, and our physical home for the unexpected. Being emotionally or mentally available can look like regularly checking in with your family and friends and listening with attention and empathy when they respond. This requires work and sacrifice, but it is important and fulfilling.

While the House of Elrond was welcoming to those in need, it was also closely safeguarded against the servants of Sauron. "Evil things did not come into that valley" is a sobering reminder of Elrond's diligence in defending Rivendell (*The Hobbit*, ch. 3). A servant of Sauron would not find safe haven in the home of Elrond; similarly, Aragorn remarked that Lothlórien should only be feared by "those who bring some evil with them" (*LOTR*, Book II, ch. 6). While an emphasis is placed on being welcoming, a refuge filled with evil is no refuge at all.

Practically, this looks like rooting out vice in our own lives and placing boundaries around what we allow into our homes and communities. Recall our discussion of stewardship and pursuit of peace, which involves rooting out injustice and abuse. Ultimately, true hospitality is always deeply rooted in love. St. Thomas Aquinas defined love as willing the good of another; in striving toward goodness for ourselves, we can also do the same for others. We can love people by making room for them. We can endure inconveniences for the sake of another. We can make ourselves available mentally by hearing about their day, spiritually by praying for them, or physically by inviting them over. Inspired by Elrond's example, we can make our homes beacons of light, shelters from storms, and houses of healing.

THE ROAD GOES ON

Introduce yourself to someone who might be new to your community. This could be a new neighbor, coworker, classmate, person at church, or someone in your online community. Be intentional about showing hospitality, and look for ways to connect them to others in your network.

Chapter 7

DISCERN YOUR PATH

Values: Clarity, Growth, Foresight, and Peace

> Good and ill have not changed since yesteryear; nor are they one thing among Elves and Dwarves and another among Men. It is a man's part to discern them, as much in the Golden Wood as in his own house.
>
> *LOTR*, Book III, ch. 2

The evening star burned brightly above the woods of Lothlórien, its light glistening across the rippling water that filled the small silver basin far below: the Mirror of Galadriel. Before it stood two hobbits—Frodo and Sam—and the elven Lady Galadriel. She offered them the chance to look into her mirror, whose water may show many things, "things that were, and things that are, and things that yet may be" (*LOTR*, Book II, ch. 7).

Through the mirror's visions, both hobbits were offered a choice. Sam the Stouthearted took the first look. In the mirror, he was faced with a vision of his master in some unknown danger, followed by a vision of his beloved Shire in peril. At this moment, he had to decide between his commitment to Frodo and his desire to return home.

When Frodo looked into the mirror, he saw scenes from the complex history in which he had become entangled, leaving him feeling that the Ring was too great a burden for someone so small. In his moment of weakness, Frodo held the simple golden band out before the wise lady of Lothlórien. Here, Galadriel herself was faced with a choice. The Ring called to her: She imagined herself a queen, not dark but beautiful, one whose dominion would begin with fair motives. But she knew it would not end there, just as Sauron's own fair motives had turned to an insatiable pursuit of control. And so, after centuries of contemplation and strengthening resolve, she would not claim it for herself.

We have examined the role of Providence in both *The Lord of the Rings* and our own lives, reflecting on how an openness to Fate will guide us along the paths of our lives. But how are we to know which path to take? The next step in this journey is one of discernment. Rather than acting on whims, emotions, or out of fear, discernment involves carefully examining your own purpose and making decisions that align with your values. From a Christian perspective, this looks like making decisions with the goal of honoring God's will for your life. Setting a strong foundation for ourselves can help us anticipate the challenges, temptations, or doubts that we might encounter along the way. Within the context of *The Lord of the Rings*, the Fellowship's time in Lothlórien can be seen as a time of discernment—for everyone involved.

Lothlórien as a Test

Lothlórien was in many ways a test for our heroes, both for the Fellowship and for Galadriel herself. In Lothlórien, Galadriel presented each of them with an escape route. They had sworn no oath and might still leave freely, and the temptation to do so may have been growing in their hearts. Tolkien writes, "All of them, it seemed, had fared alike: each had felt that he was offered a choice between a shadow full of fear that lay ahead, and something that he greatly desired: clear before his mind it lay, and to get it he had only to turn aside from the road and leave the Quest and the war against Sauron to others" (*LOTR*, Book II, ch. 7).

Each member of the Fellowship felt as if Galadriel had offered them a choice, one between paths known and unknown. In these moments, Tolkien illustrates the powerful role that temptation can play in the process of discernment as we seek to make choices that support our values and purpose.

The Ring tempted Galadriel by suggesting that with its power she would be able to supplant Sauron, setting herself up as a queen in his place. While she was regarded as the Lady of Lothlórien, she was never revered as a queen (*Letters*, 210). At the end of the Third Age, the realm of Lothlórien was preserved and protected through the power of her elven ring, Nenya, but its power was entangled with Sauron's ring.

If the One Ring were to return to Sauron's hand, the elven rings would once again be subject to Sauron's control. The elves would have to take off their rings and lose the ability to maintain their realms, prompting them to leave Middle-earth. If the One Ring were to be destroyed, the power of the elven Rings would also be lost, and the elves would diminish and return to the Blessed Realm. In offering her the One Ring, Frodo presented Galadriel with the only possible way to maintain her status in Middle-earth. But it was ultimately an impossible decision. Her original reasons for coming to Middle-earth were legitimate (*Letters*, 353), but Sauron's creation of the One Ring had bound the fate of the elves to his own. Because of Sauron's grasp for dominion, Galadriel was ultimately left without a true choice. With or without the Ring, there could be no true possibility of ruling in Middle-earth. Instead, her fate demanded a return to the Blessed Realm.

In Galadriel's rejection of the Ring, her hard-won resolve was finally put to use. She explained that she had spent many years wondering how she would respond if given the choice. Tolkien writes that her decision to reject the Ring had been made long ago, but it was only in that moment that it became final (*Letters*, 246). She had prepared herself for the temptation through discernment and was able to resist it when the chance came: She successfully rejected Frodo's offer of the Ring.

Dreams of Dominions

Throughout *The Lord of the Rings*, we meet characters who exemplify great virtue and great evil. Within each of these characters was the *potential* to become either great or evil—their choices determined who they were. Through the characters of Galadriel and Sauron, we can understand that the desire to govern is not evil. Rather, it is the disregard of the freedom of others in pursuit of domination that brings about evil. Galadriel was willing to prioritize the good of others above her own self-interest; Sauron was not.

In the beginning, the desires of Sauron and Galadriel were not too different. Sauron began with the desire "to order all things according to his own wisdom" (*Letters*, 183). Similarly, Galadriel dreamed of ruling a realm of her own. It was this desire that led her to forsake the Blessed Realm and go with the rest of her kin to Middle-earth. Galadriel "had dreams of far lands and dominions that might be her own to order as she would without tutelage" (*UT*, 222).

At the end of the First Age, Galadriel refused to return to the Blessed Realm; she was the only elf in exile to refuse the pardon of the Valar (*Silm*, ch. 24). Similarly, Sauron repented before a herald of the Valar around this same time but abandoned this pursuit when asked to return to the Blessed Realm to receive his judgment (*Silm*, Of the Rings of Power and the Third Age). Both were former servants of the Vala Aulë and possessed a keen power of insight into the minds of others. As the Second Age wore on, Sauron perceived that Galadriel would be one of his chief foes and obstacles. Because of their closeness in nature and contrast in choice, they can be seen as narrative foils. Ultimately, Sauron was willing to enslave and manipulate those he once sought to save in order to achieve his goals. Galadriel was not. Sauron's story is a descent into darkness and ruin, while Galadriel's choices caused her to grow in goodness, strength, and light. Her final rejection of the Ring illustrated the irreconcilable divide between the elves and Sauron.

Sauron's Temptation

Sauron, and by extension his Ring, did not target a person's weaknesses but rather played to their strengths. Just as Sauron himself began with noble desires and purposes, the Ring worked through fair-seeming visions. Through its power, the Ring promised its bearer would grow mighty enough to achieve an otherwise impossible end. Galadriel was tempted through her desire to rule; she would have begun with justice and light, but in her wisdom, she knew she would only serve to replace the dark lord with a new tyrant. "All shall love me and despair!" she cried to Frodo (*LOTR*, Book II, ch. 7).

The Ring called to others in a similar way. It spoke to Gandalf through his pity for the people of Middle-earth, tempting him to use it for goodness: "Yet the way of the Ring to my heart is by pity, pity for weakness and the desire of strength to do good" (*LOTR*, Book I, ch. 2). For Sam, it presented a vision of the desolate lands of Mordor transformed into a garden under his command. For Boromir, the Ring offered a weapon with which to save his people and earn renown. Each of these spoke to a noble pursuit, which would have ultimately been corrupted through the power of Sauron.

Most of the world's injustice is committed by people who do not see their actions as evil. Like Sauron, they may begin with good intentions, making slow progress toward a seemingly noble pursuit. In the same way, Sauron's Ring sought to manipulate good intentions. Being rooted in a sense of identity and purpose can provide strength in resisting temptation. But if the conscience is not carefully formed and rooted in love, even fair motives can be twisted into horrible ends. Nurturing our own sense of goodness is done by making small, daily choices that support our beliefs and convictions. For myself, these convictions are guided by Christ's call to love one another as he loved us (John 13:34).

Faithful Discernment

While Frodo and Sam would leave Lothlórien with their resolve strengthened and their minds made up, this discernment did not come so easily for all members of the Fellowship. In particular, both Boromir and Aragorn carried a sense of restlessness and indecision with them as they left Lothlórien.

The ways of the elves were strange to Boromir, and he was filled with doubt at every turn. Disregarding the wisdom of the Council of Elrond, he believed it would be folly to destroy the Ring; instead, he wanted to bring it to Gondor where it would be wielded against Sauron. Just as Boromir had wished for a plain and known path before entering into the Golden Wood, he felt that returning to Gondor with the Ring was the most obvious and straightforward choice. While his intentions were noble, his decision-making process was based on a misreading of his circumstances, and so his judgment was clouded. When Boromir's temptation reached its height, he tried to take the Ring from Frodo by force. In acting on this impulse, he caused Frodo to flee and the Fellowship to break. He quickly repented, however, and chose to heroically defend Merry and Pippin from the Uruk-hai in his final moments.

Even Aragorn, who had been raised in Rivendell and steeped in the wisdom of the elves, struggled to understand his exact path forward. Without Gandalf's leadership, Aragorn was "divided in his mind" about whether to follow Boromir to Minas Tirith as he had originally intended or to remain with Frodo as he turned toward Mordor (*LOTR*, Book II, ch. 8). Though his understanding of his ultimate identity as king remained strong, the journey to his throne remained unclear.

In the context of our own lives, we can learn from Boromir's example that even when we do fall to temptation, we can quickly correct our course and still choose to do the right thing. And we can imitate Aragorn's careful discernment and commitment to an ultimate goal. It may feel overwhelming when we are taking the first steps, but our own understanding and determination will grow with time.

Noah's Faithfulness

This theme of discernment and faithfulness to our deepest convictions takes shape in a Noah-like figure in Middle-earth. Thousands of years before *The Lord of the Rings*, Númenor represented the height of human civilization, which then brought about its own downfall through pride and rebellion against God. Both Boromir and Aragorn were descendants of Númenóreans. In the waning of Númenor, its people were divided into two factions: the King's Men and the *Elendili* ("Elf-friends"), also called the Faithful. The King's Men were estranged from the elves and the angelic beings known as the Valar and strove for immortality above all things; the Faithful remained loyal to the House of Elros (the original lineage of kings), sought friendship with the elves, and did not reject the counsel of the Valar. The Faithful were ultimately led by Elendil and his father Amandil.

Going before his son, Amandil embarked upon a secret mission to break the ban of the Valar and sail to the Blessed Realm to plead for mercy on behalf of Númenor. Though this was considered treason, Amandil felt called to do so because he believed "there is but one loyalty from which no man can be absolved in heart for any cause" (*Silm*, Akallabêth). This is a powerful reminder that our allegiance is owed to God before any kings, and that rebellion against unjust laws is fidelity to justice. Amandil was unsuccessful, however, and never returned from this voyage. It was then that Elendil and his sons foresaw Númenor's downfall and prepared to flee.

Tolkien describes Elendil as being like Noah for his people, leading them faithfully through the tribulations of a great flood (*Letters*, 156 and 131). In the biblical account, Noah had been instructed by God to build a ship in preparation for a great flood. Like Noah, Elendil's faithfulness in discernment resulted in the saving of his people and a reestablishment of Númenórean civilization after its downfall.

In carefully discerning God's will for our lives, we benefit both ourselves and those around us; in being faithful to our convictions and purpose, we can be confident that we are on the right path.

Casting Out Doubt

Overcoming temptation strengthens resolve as doubt is cast out. A person who has passed through temptation no longer needs to ask, "What would I do in this situation?"—because they now know.

Doubt left room for Sauron to bore into a person's mind; a firm resolution acted as a barrier against him. Galadriel tested the members of the company, especially Frodo and Sam, before Sauron himself could, so that they would be prepared when it happened later. As Sam and Frodo inched closer to Mount Doom and the end of their quest, their minds were made up. Sam "knew all the arguments of despair and would not listen to them. His will was set, and only death would break it" (*LOTR*, Book VI, ch. 3).

Whereas Sauron's temptation proved ruinous, the Mirror of Galadriel informed a person's decision and strengthened their resolve. After being offered the choice to turn back, both Frodo and Sam went forward with renewed determination.

Within *The Lord of the Rings*, some characters heroically resist temptation while others fall; there are lessons to be learned from each of these examples, which serve as both aspirational and cautionary tales. We will all face moments of doubt or temptation throughout our lives, and it's how we respond that determines our path.

Like Galadriel, those who would wield power must do so with humility, prudence, and self-mastery. Tolkien's heroes bring peace by resisting temptation, rooting out injustice, and defending what is good. Self-mastery brings inner peace and allows us to be good stewards. Discernment is a foundation to strong leadership; a good leader must intentionally form their conscience, so they are able to determine right from wrong.

Aragorn is also an example of prudence, the virtue that utilizes practical reason to discern what is good and the right steps toward this goodness. There are several points throughout his journey when Aragorn struggled to discern his next step forward, but because he had been diligent in his formation, he ultimately reached his destination.

In the context of our own lives, there are many ways that we can carefully form our consciences and discern our purpose. When making hard decisions, we can seek advice from those we trust. For the Christian, we can bring all these choices to the Lord in prayer as well as devote time to spiritual reading. The wisdom we find in the *Catechism of the Catholic Church* and in the written works of the saints can inform our conscience and guide us in making decisions.

In all of this, we can choose to take small actions now that will help us resist temptation with conviction when we most need strength and hope. Attending to our interior lives will bring self-mastery and inner peace. Even if this is the work of a lifetime, the small steps we take along the way add up. And we do not journey through temptation alone—God has promised to be near to us especially in these moments. He is as near as a simple prayer.

THE ROAD GOES ON

Reflect on a time you were given the choice to leave a difficult path you were on. What convictions helped you to stay the course? Looking ahead, what are some temptations you may face in the future? What practices might you take up to strengthen your resolve and clarify your purpose?

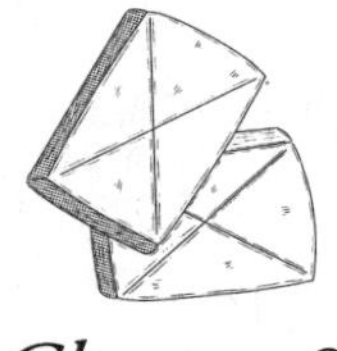

Chapter 8

EMBRACE YOUR GIFTS

Values: Adaptability, Resourcefulness, Provision, and Empowerment

> Frodo took the phial, and for a moment as it shone between them, he saw [Galadriel] again standing like a queen, great and beautiful, but no longer terrible. He bowed, but found no words to say.
>
> *LOTR*, Book II, ch. 8

It is now mid-February, and the remaining members of the Fellowship have spent a little more than a month in the woods of Lothlórien. They have each been tested and will now go forward into the darkness. Before they depart, they are given several gifts from Galadriel and Celeborn. Each gift is given with the intent of strengthening its bearer for the trials to come, in the hope of defeating Sauron.

Within Tolkien's Legendarium, we encounter many occasions for gifts, both given and received. In this chapter, we will discuss the nature of gifts in Tolkien's writing and how we can apply these same principles to our own lives. There are many ways to approach the subject of gifts: immaterial gifts such as time or talent, tangible gifts such as for a birthday or holiday, and even the gift of self in which one person is willing to cast aside their own desires for the sake of another. There are times when we ourselves will be givers of gifts, and other times when we will receive gifts. We each have unique gifts, talents, and skills—and we can recognize that life itself is the greatest gift we've been given.

Gift and Mission

A quest often begins with a gift: Our hero is equipped and sent forth. Sometimes it's a map, sometimes it's a weapon. In Frodo's case, it was a Ring. Frodo did not know it at the time, but this Ring came with a great mission.

Leaving Lothlórien marked a turning point in Frodo's quest. Whereas he had previously been able to rely on the guidance of Gandalf, he was now untethered from that security. Several possible outcomes had once seemed open to him, but now he understood only one remained. He had now begun in earnest. Soon, he and Sam would be separated from the rest of the Fellowship as they began the wandering road to Mordor. Perhaps Galadriel foresaw this. Perhaps she knew they would need the gifts of light and hope.

By taking a careful look at gifts within *The Lord of the Rings*, we can learn about the nature of gift-giving in our own world. Hobbits were accustomed to receiving and giving gifts, but Frodo could not have guessed how important the gifts of Galadriel would be. Hobbits were well-known for their peculiar but endearing habit of giving gifts to friends and relatives to celebrate one's own birthday. These gifts were often small and inexpensive, but nevertheless exciting. Hobbits were so fond of giving gifts to one another that most of their homes were quite cluttered with what they called *mathoms*, items they had no use for but were still unwilling to part with. The prevalence of *mathoms* became so widespread throughout the Shire that museums called mathom-houses were established to display important or interesting items. The most notable object in one of these mathom-houses was Bilbo's coat of mithril, which he later gave to Frodo. The lessons to be learned from hobbits regarding gifts are manifold. Gifts don't need to be expensive or valuable to be appreciated. Gifts should be given freely and without strings attached. It's okay to re-gift items you don't need anymore. It's also okay to keep around items of sentimental value even if they have no practical use. Hobbits celebrated gifts because they signified generosity and carried treasured memories.

"It is a Gift"

In the Second Age of Middle-earth, Sauron was not yet the powerful dark lord we know in *The Lord of the Rings*. Instead, he began this era of Middle-earth at a low point. After the defeat of the original dark lord Morgoth at the end of the First Age, Sauron lingered, momentarily forgotten by the Valar, the god-like beings he had once served. As he slowly returned to power, he enacted a plan to rebuild his strength: He sought to seduce the elves and, with their help, forge the Rings of Power.

In this time, Sauron put on a fair form and presented himself to the elves as Annatar, Lord of Gifts, an emissary of the Valar. The usage of the word "gifts" in his given name is worth pondering. After the creation of the Rings of Power, Eregion was ultimately destroyed and the elven-smith Celebrimbor killed by Sauron. While the elven rings were hidden, the remaining Rings of Power were taken and distributed by Sauron to both dwarves and men—as gifts.

For Tolkien, both life and death were gifts from God. In *The Lord of the Ring*s, Sauron attempted to subvert the gifts of life and death through the Rings of Power. The rings given to men prolonged their lives but also made living unbearable; they became slaves to Sauron, who held both life and death for ransom.

At the end of the Second Age, an alliance of all the free peoples of Middle-earth stood against Sauron. In this war, the Ring was ultimately cut from Sauron's finger by Isildur. Isildur kept the Ring as a *weregild*, a symbolic compensation for the loss of his father and brother at Sauron's hand. When Isildur wrote about the Ring, he called it "precious." After Isildur's death, the Ring was abandoned to the Anduin river for more than two thousand years until it was found by a hobbit named Déagol. Sméagol, his cousin, demanded the Ring be given to him as a birthday gift—and killed Déagol when he refused. Later, when Bilbo passed the Ring down to Frodo, he did so on his birthday. Because hobbits traditionally gave gifts on their birthday, it was a gift both given *and* received. In *The Fellowship of the Ring*, when Boromir was consumed by temptation for the Ring, he called it a gift (*LOTR*, Book II, ch. 10).

Tolkien presents Sauron's work through the lens of gift-giving to draw a connection to the subversion of gifts, which are meant to be freely given. Sauron's "gifts" always came with a cost and were in essence an attack against God himself as Sauron strove to manipulate Eru's plans for creation. In the context of our own lives, we should be wary of fair-seeming gifts that attempt to subvert the natural rhythm of life or that come with strings attached. Tolkien's insights also remind us what true freedom and generosity look like.

Galadriel's Gifts

For Galadriel to bestow the Fellowship with gifts was an act of defiance against the "Lord of Gifts." Given freely and out of love, her gifts ultimately aided Frodo and the rest of the Fellowship in the defeat of Sauron. Each of Galadriel's gifts was intentionally chosen according to its recipient's needs:

- To Aragorn, she gave a sheath made to fit his sword, Andúril, and the title Elessar and its corresponding brooch.
- To Boromir, she gave a gold belt.
- To Merry and Pippin, she gave small silver belts with clasps shaped like golden flowers.
- To Legolas, she gave a bow of the Galadhrim and a quiver of arrows.
- Gimli initially refused to ask for any gift, insisting that to have seen and heard the Lady Galadriel was enough of a gift. When pressed, however, he asked only for a single strand of her hair; in her generosity, she gave him three, which he vowed to set into a crystal as a "pledge of good will between the Mountain and the Wood until the end of days" (*LOTR*, Book II, ch. 8).
- To Sam, she gave a small box that held earth from her orchard and a seed to be used when he returned to his gardens.

- To Frodo, she gave a small crystal phial that held the light of Eärendil's star, saying, "May it be a light to you in dark places, when all other lights go out" (*LOTR*, Book II, ch. 8).

To all of the Fellowship, she gave lembas bread, elvish cloaks, and rope.

The Blessed Sacrament

The role of Galadriel's gift of lembas is worth exploring more. While the other gifts reflected more specialized needs, the gift of food spoke to the importance of caring for a person's basic needs. At the same time, while lembas looked like ordinary bread, it had a hidden strength that nourished both body and soul. Catholics may notice many similarities between the elvish bread and the Blessed Sacrament, and this was no coincidence.

Lembas was first given to the elves in the Blessed Realm by one of the Valar, Yavanna; similarly, the Eucharist is referred to as bread from heaven. When given to a person near to or in danger of death, the Eucharist is called *viaticum* ("provision for a journey" in Latin). Similarly, lembas was called "waybread" by the elves and was given to the members of the Fellowship as they left on their perilous trek. Tolkien acknowledged these parallels when responding to a reader who had noted the Catholic influence. He wrote, "Another saw in waybread (lembas) = viaticum and the reference to its feeding the will and being more potent when fasting, a derivation from the Eucharist" (*Letters*, 213).

The elves explained that the waybread was "given to serve you when all else fails" (*LOTR*, Book II, ch. 8). Lembas was also considered more "potent" when it was a person's sole sustenance. This might be seen as a nod to the practice of fasting for one hour before receiving Communion. And just as lembas must be eaten daily, it is recommended that Catholics receive the Blessed Sacrament often.

In lembas, the peoples of Middle-earth find renewed strength of spirit and body; it often reminds them of home or safer times. Tolkien similarly wrote of receiving Communion as "a fleeting glimpse of an unfallen world" (*Letters*, 55). We see these same ideas echoed when Merry remarks to Pippin that lembas "does put heart into you! A more wholesome sort of feeling, too" (*LOTR*, Book III, ch. 3). And the elves themselves remarked that it was "more strengthening than any food made by man" (*LOTR*, Book II, ch. 8). As Frodo and Sam came desperately close to the end of their journey, they found that lembas had "a virtue without which they would long ago have lain down to die . . . it fed the will, and it gave strength to endure, and to master sinew and limb beyond the measure of mortal kind" (*LOTR*, Book VI, ch. 3).

Catholics view the Eucharist as one of the greatest gifts a person can receive, so it is fitting that its parallel, lembas, is included in the gifts from Galadriel. In the Mass, ordinary bread and wine become the Real Presence of Jesus Christ—his body and blood, soul and divinity. For Catholics, Christ is truly and miraculously present in the Blessed Sacrament. While there is markedly no such parallel within lembas, its power to nourish both body and soul speaks to the influence of the Eucharist on Tolkien's life.

In many letters, Tolkien expressed his devotion to the Blessed Sacrament, calling it "the one great thing to love on earth" in which one would find "romance, glory, honour, fidelity, and the true way of all your loves on earth" (*Letters*, 43). Rereading *The Lord of the Rings* for the first time after becoming Catholic was an illuminating experience, as the symbolism of lembas suddenly became apparent to me. Just as Tolkien's works had always deepened my appreciation for the natural world, I soon found myself growing in devotion to the Blessed Sacrament as well. Much like the way lembas buoyed the Fellowship over the course of their journey, the Blessed Sacrament has become a life raft for me through many storms.

Gifts of the Holy Spirit

St. Thomas Aquinas was a thirteenth-century Dominican priest and theologian whose writings, primarily his *Summa Theologica* ("The Summary of Theology"), profoundly influenced Western philosophy and theology. Jonathan McIntosh argues in *The Flame Imperishable: Tolkien, St. Thomas, and the Metaphysics of Faerie* that Aquinas was one of the foremost influences on Tolkien's metaphysical imagination.

Indeed, Tolkien's understanding of virtue, creation, free will, and evil seem to have their basis in Aquinas's framework. Tolkien's personal library included a seven-volume *Summa Theologica*; he also owned and left handwritten notes in the Thomistic philosopher Jacques Maritain's 1942 *Introduction to Philosophy*.

Tolkien's understanding of creation, in particular, is reminiscent of Thomistic philosophy. Both Tolkien and Aquinas believed it is a gift to have been created and that our own creative acts further adorn God's handiwork. Aquinas taught that all good gifts originate from God, who is the source of all goodness. Tolkien expressed this concept as "sub-creation"—the idea that, as creatures, our own creativity is a participation in God's life and generosity.

The Christian life is nourished by gifts as well—consider the gifts of the Holy Spirit: wisdom to perceive God's will, understanding truth, right judgment, courage, knowledge of God's creation, reverence for God, and a sense of wonder and awe. In fact, Aquinas even suggested that "Gift" could serve as a name for God because of the role the Holy Spirit plays in our lives.

Giving and Receiving Gifts

In the context of our own lives, we might draw many lessons from the gifts of Galadriel. Each of her gifts was given with thought and intention, prompting us to do the same when giving gifts to one another. They also illustrate the power of gift-giving to both provide material aid and lift a person's spirits. In providing food or shelter to the hungry or unhoused, for example, we are also affirming their dignity and entering into a shared human experience with them. In the same way that Galadriel equipped the travelers for their journeys ahead, we can be inspired to take special care for the refugee. To a smaller degree, we can also consider hosting or attending communal events such as a gift exchange, potluck, or a book discussion. These types of events allow everyone involved to share their own unique talents, perspectives, and gifts with others.

The gifts of Galadriel show us what it means to give gifts with purpose and care. They also show us what it looks like to accept the mission that can come with a gift. How do we respond when we receive gifts? We might write thank-you notes, we might allow the gift to lead us to new perspectives or experiences, we might cherish the gift and what it represents. When given a gift, we should respond with action and gratitude. We can also respond by becoming givers of gifts in return.

The gifts of Sauron always came with a price—they worked toward the benefit of the one who gave them. By contrast, a true gift should be given for the well-being of the recipient. Gifts should be given unselfishly. To learn to give selflessly can be one of life's greatest lessons and will strengthen your relationships throughout your life.

The gifts we have given and received in our lives—especially the invisible gifts of love and support from those close to us—can be transformative, equipping and orienting each of us for the journey of our lives. When we nurture the gifts we have been given—both in the natural sense of talents, skills, and passions, as well as the spiritual sense of the gifts of the Holy Spirit—we are continuing God's good work.

THE ROAD GOES ON

Give a gift to someone in your life. Choose your recipient carefully, and consider what might be useful or otherwise life-giving to them in their season of life. The purpose of this exercise is not to spend money or give something mass-produced or wasteful, but instead to give from the heart. For this exercise, it is the thought that counts. You have a budget of ten dollars. Who will you choose and what will you give? What is the purpose behind this gift?

Chapter 9

Awaken Your Courage

Values: Courage, Bravery, Stoutness of Heart, and Steadiness

> Éowyn it was, and Dernhelm also. For into Merry's mind flashed the memory of the face that he saw at the riding from Dunharrow: the face of one that goes seeking death, having no hope. Pity filled his heart and great wonder, and suddenly the slow-kindled courage of his race awoke. He clenched his hand. She should not die, so fair, so desperate! At least she should not die alone, unaided.
>
> *LOTR*, Book V, ch. 6

The clanging of steel blades rings in Merry's ears. The air is heavy with dread as he stands in the midst of a great battle in the Pelennor Fields. No taller than a child, the hobbit is overlooked as the fighting rages on. He is overwhelmed, wondering what madness drove him to think he could accomplish any great deeds in a war so much bigger than him. But then he sees her: Éowyn stands before the Witch-king of Angmar, and she laughs. Her golden hair shines in the sun as she raises her blade in defiance. Though no living man might hinder a foe so deadly, she is no man.

I do not consider myself to be a particularly brave person. Actually, I'd say I'm an extremely anxious person. Most things scare me, most things make me nervous. But here's the important part: I have learned to do difficult things anyway. (Writing this book is one of those things; I have found this entire process terrifying. And yet here we are, together!)

Throughout my life, I have made a conscious effort to be receptive to opportunities that come my way even if they scare me. Like Bilbo, I don't go seeking out adventure—I don't seek out any adventures at all! I don't want to leave my cozy life, and I don't want to be late for dinner. I don't enjoy public speaking or sharing a piece of myself online. I don't like being away from home or receiving attention at events. But I believe sharing my passion and insights about Tolkien is a part of my purpose somehow, so I have tried to remain faithful to that calling no matter how scary it might be. Sometimes I feel like I'm being pulled kicking and screaming down the path of my life, but I keep going anyway. I try my best to trust that Providence will guide me, all the while drawing courage from the eternal.

In pursuing this calling, I have grown in my own understanding of both Tolkien and myself. I've met some of my dearest friends because of the Tea with Tolkien community and have had some unforgettable experiences. Much like Bilbo, my life has been changed by this journey (although, thankfully, I have not acquired any evil magic jewelry!). With each speaking engagement or interview, I have grown in confidence, preparing myself for whatever opportunities the future may hold.

"Be Gone If You Be Not Deathless"

Éowyn's courage in facing the Witch-king inspires me to courage daily. The niece of king Théoden, Éowyn of Rohan was descended from a long legacy of valor and heroism. She and her brother were raised by the king after the death of their parents. While she was greatly loved and well cared for, Éowyn grew up with an identity that was founded on valor and renown.

When the time came for Rohan to ride to battle, Éowyn was left to rule at Meduseld in Théoden's stead until the men would return. Háma had advocated for Éowyn to rule in Théoden's place, saying, "She is fearless and high-hearted. All love her. Let her be as lord to the Eorlingas, while we are gone" (*LOTR*, Book III, ch. 6). This duty was a charge of great honor and responsibility, yet ultimately little glory. It was high praise but earned her only a temporary role that would be removed upon the return of the men from battle; it brought little security or renown. She was restless, worrying that her life was wasting away.

To Aragorn, Éowyn confessed that she feared most of all a cage; what she desired above all was the freedom to live her life well and fully. In Aragorn, she saw "a hope of glory and great deeds, and lands far from the fields of Rohan" (*LOTR*, Book V, ch. 8). She had hoped that a union with Aragorn would provide her with a means out of her situation, but she ultimately felt the sting of his refusal. When no one would allow her to ride into battle, she abandoned her charge and followed them anyway.

Without hope of victory in life, Éowyn rode in pursuit of glory in death. But in doing so, she was able to serve her people in a way that would have never been possible had she remained home. And though she felt hopeless and rode with a desire for death in battle, she brought with her the strength to defend her people and king. Standing before the Nazgûl king, Éowyn was prepared to lose her own life for the protection of Théoden—but in a stunning turn of events, she was victorious. The reign of terror caused by Sauron's greatest servant had ended.

Marian Strength

Éowyn's act of cutting off the head of the Nazgûl king's winged beast evokes the image of Mary, who is often portrayed crushing the head of a snake representing Satan. This depiction makes a reference to the biblical account of humanity's fall in Genesis when the serpent deceives Adam and Eve. As a result, God promises that the woman's offspring would one day crush the serpent's head. In the Christian tradition, Jesus is seen as a "new Adam" and Mary a "new Eve" because of their roles in redeeming humanity. Both Éowyn and Mary reveal that feminine strength is not docile or dainty—it is powerful enough to change the course of history.

Éowyn has also been compared to St. Joan of Arc for her courage in battle. Her words to the Nazgûl king are a powerful call to valor. In the moment when all others quailed before him, she stood bravely. Her cry can be seen as an anthem for holding fast to courage and rejecting fear: "You stand between me and my lord and kin. Begone, if you be not deathless! For living or dark undead, I will smite you, if you touch him" (*LOTR*, Book V, ch. 6). This daring proclamation is a defining moment for her character, and I have carried her specific phrases into my own life:

- "You stand between me and my lord and kin" is a call to defeat the things that stand between me and my values.
- "Begone, if you be not deathless!" can be read as a rejection of death as I strive to root my courage in the hope of eternity.
- "For living or dark undead, I will smite you, if you touch him" is an appeal to devout courage and abandonment to love.

All of Éowyn's life had been building to this moment. Similarly, all of the principles we have discussed so far have also been building toward this moment in *your* life. Éowyn shows us that we have what we need to be heroes right here and now—we can find heroic courage within our own sense of identity and purpose, no matter what circumstances of life we are facing. Éowyn's actions might have been seen as reckless, but because of her deeply held convictions, she was ultimately triumphant. A carefully laid foundation is able to withstand storms. If you have carefully formed your interior life, you can trust your gut. If your convictions lead you in one direction, follow them boldly.

Éowyn's courage, in turn, kindled courage in Merry, propelling him to stab the Witch-king. The small hobbit had gone unnoticed on the battlefield and now stood blinking in the sunlight, overcome with a love for Éowyn and a conviction that she should not die unaided. Tolkien wrote there was a "seed of courage hidden (often deeply, it is true) in the heart of the fattest and most timid hobbit, waiting for some final and desperate danger to make it grow" (*LOTR*, Book I, ch. 8). Like Éowyn, Merry had been told that he was not suited for the battlefield, and yet together they withstood one of Sauron's greatest servants. Merry was able to wound the Witch-king because he had followed his path with faithfulness, and Fate had brought this particular blade into his hand for this exact moment. As the Witch-king drew himself back to kill Éowyn, Merry stabbed him in the leg. This blade was imbued with the power to break the magic that preserved the Witch-king, "cleaving the undead flesh, breaking the spell that knit his unseen sinews to his will" (*LOTR*, Book V, ch. 6). In turn, this gave Éowyn the opportunity to plunge her sword into his helm, killing him.

Like Éowyn, our actions have the power to inspire others toward heroic courage and action. Éowyn's victory was not possible without Merry—two people who were not supposed to be on the battlefield turned the tide in favor of victory. Éowyn's courage kindled Merry's heart, and together they did something that no one else could have.

While Tolkien wrote that he did not consider himself courageous, he did serve alongside other brave soldiers during the First World War (*Letters*, 43). Later in his life, Tolkien faced professional criticism for writing fantasy, which was deemed escapist and childish. Yet, he courageously defended the value of myth and Faerie, arguing that such stories explored profound truths about humanity and morality. This defense was a professional risk, similar to Faramir's moral courage in the War of the Ring. Faramir resisted his society's focus on power and military might, choosing instead what he saw as morally honorable, mirroring Tolkien's determination to champion his intellectual convictions despite academic opposition.

Éowyn's story did not end on the Pelennor Fields. After her defeat of the Witch-king, she was taken to the Houses of Healing, where she would slowly but surely recover from her wounds. There, she would also grow to understand herself more fully, discerning her vocations to become a healer and to marry Faramir: "Then the heart of Éowyn changed, or else at last she understood it. And suddenly her winter passed, and the sun shone on her" (*LOTR*, Book VI, ch. 5).

We have gotten this far into the journey by firmly planting our feet on the ground and rooting ourselves in the values that we want our lives to reflect. Inspired by Éowyn's courage, we can strive to understand our own hearts and find there a wellspring of courage. Once you've done that, you will find that you can trust yourself and your convictions to take big steps to follow Éowyn, who was guided by her courage through darkness and headfirst into the shining sun.

THE ROAD GOES ON

Reflect on examples of courage—either from people you know or from historical figures. Think of at least three people you admire: What is it about them that inspires you? How can their example prompt you to action? What is one situation in your life right now that requires courage—and how can you summon the strength to respond?

Chapter 10

Anchor Yourself in Hope

Values: Hope, Fortitude, Optimism, and Groundedness

> There, peeping among the cloud-wrack above a dark tor high up in the mountains, Sam saw a white star twinkle for a while. The beauty of it smote his heart, as he looked up out of the forsaken land, and hope returned to him. For like a shaft, clear and cold, the thought pierced him that in the end the Shadow was only a small and passing thing: there was light and high beauty for ever beyond its reach.
>
> *LOTR*, Book VI, ch. 2

Two small and weary hobbits journey across the plains of Mordor. A sense of dread stifles the air, and the shadow threatens to drown out all hope. But beyond the power of Sauron shines the stars in the night sky. As Sam Gamgee lifts his tired eyes away from the broken earth of Mordor, his attention is drawn to a single star twinkling against the backdrop of darkness. Though he does not know this star's name or story, its very presence is enough to fill his heart with enough hope to carry on. Though it is never explicitly stated, it can be inferred that this is the star of Eärendil itself: Gil-Estel, the Star of High Hope. This star has a great history, and this moment was not the first or last time it would bring hope to a weary world.

In this chapter, we will examine the theme of hope in *The Lord of the Rings*, reflecting on its power against despair in both Middle-earth and our own world. In many ways, *The Lord of the Rings* is fundamentally a story about hope—the narrative is built around the darkness of Sauron's evil growing over the land, and the flickering glimmer of resilience in the smallest of creatures that persevered to defeat it. One reason this epic tale has endured and become a classic—and will be beloved for generations to come—is the way it reveals a path through despair. We navigate that path through our own efforts, just as the Fellowship does, yet Tolkien also shows us how Providence supports our faithfulness in unseen and mysterious ways. Let's explore with more detail the nature of hope in *The Lord of the Rings* so that we can anchor our lives in this virtue.

Our Most Beloved Star

In the center of his story world, Tolkien places a symbol of hope: a star whose light glimmers in the darkness.

The Silmarillion recounts the tale of Eärendil, the half-elven Mariner who sailed to the Blessed Realm to plead with the Valar to save Middle-earth from Morgoth. On his journey, he was guided by the light of a Silmaril that his wife Elwing bore. It had been prophesied by the elves that one day a messenger would sail to the Blessed Realm and call upon the aid of the Valar. And Eärendil came, not for his own sake, but on behalf of both elves and men whom he represented with his half-elven lineage. Ultimately, his call was heeded by the Valar, and Morgoth was defeated.

Eärendil and Elwing were not permitted to return to Middle-earth after coming to the Blessed Realm, however. Because both Eärendil and Elwing had descended from unions of elves and men, they were granted the ability to choose which race to be counted among: to be immortal as the elves or mortal as men. Elwing first chose to be counted among the elves, and for her sake Eärendil chose the same. Eärendil's ship Vingilot was hallowed and set into the sky where he would sail across the heavens with the Silmaril upon his brow like a star. This star was seen as a sign of hope for all those who remained in Middle-earth, and they named it Gil-Estel, the Star of High Hope. Its light and high beauty remained a steadfast beacon of hope throughout the remainder of Tolkien's Legendarium.

The light from this star was contained in the phial of Galadriel that guided Frodo and Sam through Shelob's tunnel. When Frodo held it aloft, he cried out, *"Aiya Eärendil elenion ancalima!"* ("Hail Eärendil, brightest of the Stars!") (*LOTR*, Book IV, ch. 9). Before this light, Shelob quailed. Tolkien wrote, "No brightness so deadly had ever afflicted [Shelob's eyes] before. From sun and moon and star they had been safe underground, but now a star had descended into the very earth" (*LOTR*, Book IV, ch. 9). Even within the wastes of Mordor, Eärendil's star shone as a sign of hope for the hobbits.

While Eärendil was not meant as an allegory for Christ, nor does he represent God incarnate within Middle-earth, his character is one in which readers may find many reflected glimpses of Christ. In representing both elf and man, mortal and immortal, Eärendil is reminiscent of Christ's dual nature as both man and God. Just as Christ ascended into heaven after the Resurrection, Eärendil also ascended into the heavens.

In fact, the origins of this character actually came from a poem about Christ. The character of Eärendil and his voyages were inspired, in part, by a collection of Old English poems called *Crist* ("Christ"). These poems are about Christ's coming, Ascension, and return for the Final Judgment. They are believed to have been written around the year 800 and were preserved in a codex of Old English poetry known as the Exeter Book.

One of the poems begins in a way that will sound very familiar to readers of *The Silmarillion*: "Hail Earendel, brightest of angels / Sent to men over middle-earth" (*Christ I*). These words are mirrored in the herald Eönwë's proclamation upon Eärendil's arrival in the Blessed Realm: "Hail Eärendil, of mariners most renowned, the looked for that cometh at unawares, the longed for that cometh beyond hope! Hail Eärendil, bearer of light before the Sun and Moon! Splendour of the Children of Earth, star in the darkness, jewel in the sunset, radiant in the morning!" (*Silm*, ch. 24).

Tolkien was struck by this Old English poem—it was in many ways the beginning of his Legendarium. In his biography of Tolkien, Humphrey Carpenter wrote, "This notion of the star-mariner whose ship leaps into the sky had grown from the reference to 'Earendel' in the Cynewulf lines. But the poem that it produced was entirely original. It was in fact the beginning of Tolkien's own mythology" (*Biography*, 94).

Eärendil was a character whose fate compelled him to do great deeds, and his legacy lived on to bring hope to the weary world. He was called to plead before the powers of the world for its salvation. Because of Eärendil, one of the Silmarils was preserved forever. Eärendil's star was a sign of hope enshrined above the Shadows of Sauron and was something completely out of his reach.

St. Brendan the Navigator

Along with Eärendil's Old English inspiration, Tolkien also drew inspiration for such an otherworldly voyage from the legend of St. Brendan the Navigator.

St. Brendan was a sixth-century Irish monk, later regarded as one of the Twelve Apostles of Ireland. In addition to founding several monasteries throughout Ireland, he is most known for the sea voyages that earned him the title of "Navigator." According to the *Navigatio Sancti Brendani*, his travels included a seven-year journey across the Atlantic Ocean to the Americas in search of the "Isle of the Blessed" or the "Promised Land of the Saints." The tale of Brendan's voyages is an epic full of fantastical details and adventure—it captivated Tolkien's imagination.

Tolkien wrote a poem about the death of St. Brendan, which he titled simply "Imram" (in Irish, "Voyage"). It was published in 1955 in a British magazine called *Time and Tide*; later, Christopher Tolkien included it in *Sauron Defeated*, volume 9 of *The History of Middle-earth* series, as a part of *The Notion Club Papers*, which was

Tolkien's attempt at writing a time travel novel in which modern-day protagonists "discover" Númenor through dreams. While Tolkien ultimately abandoned the novel, the concepts therein later grew to become the story of Númenor, as published in *The Silmarillion*.

Readers familiar with *The Silmarillion* may recognize a few themes in Tolkien's poem about St. Brendan, most notably the idea of a deathless land in the West and a brilliant star that guides characters along invisible paths. The star was seen at "the parting of the ways . . . where the round world plunges steeply down, but on the old road goes as an unseen bridge that on arches runs to coasts that no man knows" (*Sauron Defeated*, *Notion Club Papers*, Part Two). The description of an "unseen bridge" is closely related to Tolkien's description of a "Straight Road" across which elves were permitted to travel through the sky to the Blessed Realm after the reshaping of the world (*Silm*, Of the Rings of Power and the Third Age). Though not named in the poem, this star can be understood as the star of Eärendil, bringing both hope and guidance to St. Brendan on his journey to paradise. These examples of Tolkien working elements of Christian tradition and legend into his own myth underscore the way that each supports the other; by weaving these symbols into his Legendarium, Tolkien illustrates the power of supernatural hope through story.

The Elvish Words for Hope: Amdir and Estel

Tolkien's elves had two words for hope: *amdir* and *estel*. *Amdir* meant "looking up," to have optimism or an expectation of goodness that has its foundation in experience. *Estel*, on the other hand, meant "trust"; to have *estel* was to have faith that extends beyond lived experience. But more than that, *estel* spoke to a relationship between a creator and creature; *estel* was trust that Ilúvatar would not create the world only for it to end in ruin.

Toward the end of *Morgoth's Ring*, the twelfth volume of the History of Middle-earth, Tolkien included a short chapter entitled "Athrabeth Finrod ah Andreth." The chapter describes a conversation between the elf Finrod and a human woman named Andreth about the nature of mortality and death. Over the course of their debate, both come to understand the fate of the other more keenly; man's fear and resentment of death is contextualized by the longevity of the elvish lifespan. In this conversation, Finrod explains the elvish concept of *estel*:

> It is not defeated by the ways of the world, for it does not come from experience, but from our nature and first being. If we are indeed the Eruhin, the Children of the One, then he will not suffer himself to be deprived of his own, not by any enemy, not even by ourselves. This is the last foundation of Estel, which we keep even when we contemplate the end: of all his designs the issue must be for his children's joy. (*Morgoth's Ring*, Athrabeth Finrod ah Andreth)

The Athrabeth is an example of Tolkien's Catholic faith clearly guiding the metaphysical framework of Arda. In addition to their discussion of hope mirroring Christian belief, Andreth later mentions a prophecy that God himself would enter into the world to redeem it: "They say that the One will himself enter into Arda, and heal Men and all the Marring from the beginning to the end" (*Morgoth's Ring*, Athrabeth Finrod ah Andreth). Though Andreth herself doesn't understand or fully believe in this sign of hope, it speaks to the belief that hope can be found by looking toward eternity because there is something else at work—something striving for our good—beyond what can be seen. Just as the elves must travel along the unseen road, hope requires a faith in things that sometimes cannot be seen or fully understood.

Sam Gamgee as the Exemplar of Hope

So many characters within *The Lord of the Rings* ultimately succeeded by simply plodding on; despite a loss of worldly hope, they held onto an "otherworldly" hope. In Sam Gamgee, I find an exemplar of hope as a virtue. He was anchored by love with the stoutest of hearts and a mind grounded in "plain hobbitsense." Even as all hope seems utterly lost, it never truly dies in the heart of Sam Gamgee. Sam's plain hobbitsense was like a firewall built around his heart that kept the flames of despair at bay. He was resolute, vowing that he would "get there, if I leave everything but my bones behind. . . . And I'll carry Mr. Frodo up myself, if it breaks my back and heart" (*LOTR*, Book VI, ch. 3).

Some people think of hope as a delicate flower that can be crushed or withered or torn out petal by petal. But hope is not so fragile. Hope is a star shining high above all doubt, a star that burns with the power of a thousand years' strength. Hope holds the stories of the past and whispers a promise for the future. Hope is the stern face of one potato-farming hobbit covered in dirt and sweat, eyes blinded with tears, taking just one more step forward into the darkness.

In his hope, Sam was the embodiment of fortitude, the virtue that nourishes a firm resolve and a constant pursuit of goodness. Fortitude turns the soft heart of a hobbit into stone and steel against weariness, despair, and doubt. In my own life, I have found that fortitude has given me the strength to carry on despite a sometimes-overwhelming amount of grief or anxiety. A person who has fortitude does not avoid suffering (as none of us can) but faces it with courage and hope. In the same way that Sam's hope was strengthened by the twinkling of Eärendil's star, we can also make a habit of looking for signs of hope in our daily lives. This does not erase our experience of suffering or injustice but reframes our perspective and strengthens our hearts.

Despair as the Enemy's Weapon

Tolkien was a man well acquainted with the temptation to despair. Like many, he struggled with bouts of melancholy throughout his life. The loss of his mother deeply grieved him and often left Tolkien with a nagging sense of impending ruin. He felt in these moments that "nothing was safe. Nothing would last. No battle would be won forever" (*Biography*, 44). Yet despite it all, he never fully gave in to despair, always seeking out moments of beauty and hope among the ruins.

For Tolkien's villains, there was a weapon more powerful than any smith might forge—one that yielded to neither sword nor shield: despair. Despair can bring a great warrior to his knees more surely than starvation and more swiftly than an arrow. Despair whispers to its foes of a battle already lost, planting seeds of hopelessness that bloom in doubt's darkness.

The chief lieutenant of Sauron—the chief of the Nazgûl, the Witch-king of Angmar whom Gandalf called "the Captain of Despair"—wielded this weapon (*LOTR*, Book V, ch. 4). As the hosts of Mordor besieged the great city of Minas Tirith during the War of the Ring, Tolkien writes, "For yet another weapon, swifter than hunger, the Lord of the Dark Tower had: dread and despair" (*LOTR*, Book V, ch. 4). The taunting presence of the Nazgûl loomed above the city, darkening the hearts of its inhabitants with thoughts of "hiding and crawling, and death" (*LOTR*, Book V, ch. 4). The mind of Denethor, ruling steward of Gondor, was ultimately strangled by the vines of despair. He had unknowingly watered them himself for years while they slowly grew up around him. He had become obsessed with the palantir, a seeing stone that presented him with a distorted perspective of the war—that Sauron's victory was imminent. Despair became a crutch for the steward, something easier and more comfortable to cling to than hope. In the end, Denethor clung to the now-familiar security that despair promised him over the risk of hope. This attachment is underscored in the moment of Denethor's death, "clasping the palantir with both hands upon his breast. And it was said that ever after, if any man looked in that Stone, unless he had a great strength of will to turn it to other purpose, he saw only two aged hands withering in flame" (*LOTR*, Book V, ch. 7). Like his son Boromir, he desired a plain and known path even if the cost would be greater. Ultimately, Denethor chose to ensure his own death rather than suffer the uncertainty of the future.

After Denethor's abandonment of both duty and reason, Gandalf ultimately took command of Minas Tirith's defenses. Here, Gandalf rekindled the flame of hope within the hearts of Gondor's quaking soldiers. When the Gate of Minas Tirith was finally broken, the Lord of the Nazgûl strode forth into the city and all fled in terror before him—all but one. There stood Gandalf, unwavering, commanding him to leave. Here, Gandalf shows us that it is not in great power or magic that despair is conquered, but in steadfast resistance.

Despair promises certainty, whereas hope lives in the unknown. It can be uncomfortable to dare to hope—it can feel foolish or too much of a risk. The temptation to resign oneself to the apparent certainty of defeat may feel more pragmatic, or so we tell ourselves.

Where There's Life, There's Hope

Across the wide plains of Rohan small white flowers called Simbelmynë dotted the tall grass, blooming in bunches across the graves of the fallen. They bloomed all year long, a symbol of life in defiance of death. Similarly, Frodo and Sam encountered a broken and forgotten statue of a king as they came closer to Mordor. Across the king's head trailed a plant with small flowers like white stars, growing across its brow like a crown. Frodo and Sam were heartened by this view, causing Frodo to exclaim, "They cannot conquer for ever!" (*LOTR*, Book IV, ch. 7).

Tolkien often used imagery of the natural world to illustrate the goodness or desolation of a region. Where plant life grew, hope was alive; where the land was barren, evil was often to blame. One of my favorite small moments in *The Silmarillion* occurs while Angband, Morgoth's fortress, was under siege. Tolkien writes that "there were green things even among the pits and broken rocks before the doors of hell" (*Silm*, ch. 14). Just like the star twinkling high above the desolation of Mordor, these growing plants spoke to the resilience of the earth against evil, of the power of life over death. Whereas evil hastens and spreads death, goodness nurtures life.

Just as a plant thrives with regular watering, we have to tend to our own sense of hope daily. This might mean starting a gratitude journal, making a habit of acknowledging the good moments of each day, setting goals and taking steps toward them, or learning new skills that encourage hope (such as gardening). It is up to each of us to water our own hope so that when the storm comes, our hope can be a steadfast shelter.

THE ROAD GOES ON

Where there is life, there is hope. In honor of Sam Gamgee, plant a seed. This could look like planting an herb in a pot that you can grow on a windowsill, purchasing a small house plant, or tending a vegetable plant in the yard. When you water the plant, remember to water your own hope.

Chapter 11

RELY ON MERCY

Values: Mercy, Understanding, Stillness, and Clemency

For now that I see him, I do pity him.
LOTR, Book IV, ch. 1

Frodo and Sam scramble across jagged stones and brambles, lost on their journey to Mordor. After pursuing their company for days, Gollum has finally come upon the hobbits. They capture Gollum, deciding to take him in as their guide to Mordor. Whereas Frodo had been previously revolted by descriptions of Gollum, he was now face-to-face with the reality of someone so disfigured by the power of the Ring. He soon remembers the wisdom of Gandalf and Bilbo, and pity for Gollum swells in his heart. This pity would anchor Frodo in all of his interactions with Gollum. And though he does not yet know it, this mercy would save all of them in the end.

The Lord of the Rings is a story steeped in mercy. It was a foundational virtue for Tolkien's own life as well as his Legendarium. All of his heroes are merciful, whereas his villains scorn mercy. Even when mercy looks like "folly," as it did when Gollum escaped from the elves or when Sam allowed Gollum to live, it ultimately proves good because it leaves room for Providence to step in and act.

There is a passivity to mercy that allows a person to cooperate more fully with Providence, though it should not be confused with inaction. Mercy simply leaves room in any circumstance for Providence; mercy says, *I am not the supreme judge and so I will leave final judgment to God's authority.* Pity is mercy put into practice when experienced as an emotion; pity moves us to intervene on behalf of mercy. In Tolkien's worldview, mercy and pity are not optional qualities for people who want to be nice—they are foundational dispositions that make us human.

Frodo's journey was one guided by mercy. Though most hobbits were not wicked or cruel to one another, mercy to any kind of heroic degree was, at first, an abstract concept to Frodo. When listening to Gandalf's account of Gollum's history, he found he was scandalized by Bilbo's pity for him, unable to understand it. He remarked that it was a pity Bilbo had not slain him when he had the chance. Gandalf's response set the tone for Frodo's entire journey and never left Frodo's heart: "Pity? It was pity that stayed his hand. Pity, and mercy: not to strike without need. And he has been well rewarded, Frodo. Be sure that he took so little hurt from the evil, and escaped in the end, because he began his ownership of the Ring so. With pity" (*LOTR*, Book I, ch. 2).

After the destruction of the Ring, Frodo returned home with a keen understanding of mercy. What once seemed a foreign concept had now become a lived reality for Frodo, who had advocated for mercy even as the hobbits expelled Saruman's ruffians from their midst. Now, on the doorstep of Bag End, he would even pity Saruman after he had tried to kill him.

There can be a temptation to demonize or scorn those who look, think, or live differently than us, but it's important to remember that we are all children of the same God. This truth calls us to allow mercy to guide all of our actions with others. Having mercy on someone else means pursuing justice while, at the same time, recognizing that we are not the supreme judge. Conversely, accepting someone else's mercy requires a great deal of humility. In this way, pride is the enemy of mercy. Throughout our lives, we will find ourselves on both the giving and receiving ends of mercy, and we forget its value and worth at our own peril. Frodo only understood pity and mercy after he encountered Gollum for himself; sometimes, it takes a lived experience to develop empathy for others. Like Frodo, we may find mercy a difficult concept at first, but our lived experience and empathy can help us grow in the virtue that allows us to participate with Providence.

The Tragedy of Sméagol

The need for pity and the efficacy of mercy was exhibited most strongly in the character of Gollum. He was once called Sméagol, a Stoorish hobbit who lived along the banks of the Anduin river in the late Third Age. On his thirty-third birthday, the year when hobbits typically came of age, Sméagol was out fishing with his cousin Déagol. Déagol was pulled into the water by a large fish where he came across a curious golden ring. Sméagol was immediately drawn to the Ring and demanded it as a birthday present from Déagol. When Déagol refused, Sméagol strangled him and hid his body.

When Sméagol returned home, he discovered that no one could see him while he wore the Ring. He used this invisibility for wicked and cruel purposes. The Ring played to his natural tendencies for snooping and digging in holes. Eventually, Sméagol was disowned by his family because of his wickedness. He wandered, alone and friendless, until he came to the Misty Mountains. There, he hid in the darkness for more than four hundred years. (As an aside, I have always found Sméagol's age of great interest because Frodo was also thirty-three when he inherited the Ring from Bilbo; and most Christians will recognize that Christ was thirty-three when he suffered, died, and rose from the dead.)

Hundreds of years later, Bilbo Baggins would find himself lost in these same mountains and, in the most curious chance of Fate, in sudden possession of this golden Ring. After trading riddles in the dark, Bilbo escaped from a very hungry and angry Gollum, and ultimately returned home to the Shire. There the Ring would remain for more than fifty years. Despite his hatred of the sun, Gollum's covetousness for the Ring compelled him to leave the mountains in search of Bilbo. He eventually found the Fellowship in Moria and pursued the hobbits until he was caught by Frodo and Sam and taken as their guide.

Over the course of his journey, Frodo would learn pity for Gollum in a poignant way that underscored Tolkien's own belief in mercy. As the Ring slowly gnawed at Frodo's heart, he began to comprehend Gollum in a way that no other could. In treating Gollum with understanding, he was also able to treat *himself* with understanding. Because of their shared experience, Frodo developed empathy with Gollum. To have hope for Gollum was to have hope for himself.

As Gollum guided Frodo and Sam toward Mount Doom, he was at war with himself. To illustrate this interior conflict, Tolkien described Gollum with a glint in his eye—his eyes were normally gray, but a green gleam appeared in Gollum's eyes whenever he was plotting wickedness. He debated himself aloud, arguing between Sméagol the halfling and Gollum the wicked creature he had become. Gollum protested that the hobbits should be killed and the Ring reclaimed; Sméagol argued that the hobbits had been kind to him and that he made an oath to his master. Eventually, the desire for the Ring was so strong that the wicked part of his heart won out. Gollum decided that he would lead Frodo and Sam to the great spider Shelob's tunnel, where she would kill them and he could claim the Ring for himself. Despite Frodo's mercy and empathy, Gollum was ultimately drawn back into the ways of evil.

Near-Repentance and Pity Scorned

Throughout his Legendarium, Tolkien highlights three characters who momentarily waver on the edge of repentance before ultimately turning aside and pursuing their own downfall wholeheartedly: Sauron, the Númenórean king Ar-Pharazôn, and Gollum.

First was Sauron, who pleaded for pardon before the herald of the Valar after Morgoth's defeat. When summoned to return to the Blessed Realm to receive his judgment, he instead "hid himself in Middle-earth" (*Silm*, Of the Rings of Power and the Third Age). It was ultimately out of fear and shame that Sauron fled, being unwilling to return in humiliation and receive a difficult penance. Here, Sauron turned from the potential of mercy of the Valar because he feared its cost. In the end, he fell back into the ways of Morgoth, following "like a shadow of Morgoth and a ghost of his malice, and walked behind him on the same ruinous path down into the Void" (*Silm*, Valaquenta).

Sauron was not content to merely bring about his own downfall and ushered countless others to their death alongside him. His hatred for the Númenóreans drove him to hasten their downfall, watering the seeds of envy and pride in their king, Ar-Pharazôn, until he was mad enough to make war against the Valar. As Ar-Pharazôn looked upon the shores of the Blessed Realm, "his heart misgave him," and he momentarily wavered (*Silm*, Akallabêth). In the end, he was too prideful and afraid to repent, and Númenor was destroyed.

Toward the end of Gollum's life, he similarly experienced a moment of near-repentance. As Gollum guided Frodo and Sam up the stairs of Cirith Ungol, he inched closer and closer to the completion of his plan to regain the Ring for himself. As was his habit, Gollum went off to sneak and plot. While he was gone, the two hobbits fell into an untroubled sleep. Tolkien describes the moment when he returns:

> A strange expression passed over his lean hungry face. The gleam faded from his eyes, and they went dim and grey, old and tired. A spasm of pain seemed to twist him, and he turned away, peering back up towards the pass, shaking his head, as if engaged in some interior debate. Then he came back, and slowly putting out a trembling hand, very cautiously he touched Frodo's knee—but almost the touch was a caress. For a fleeting moment, could one of the sleepers have seen him, they would have thought that they beheld an old weary hobbit, shrunken by the years that had car-

> ried him far beyond his time, beyond friends and kin, and the fields and streams of youth, an old starved pitiable thing. (*LOTR*, Book IV, ch. 8)

Gollum's gentle gesture marked his own moment of near-repentance. But Sam awoke and rebuked him; Tolkien refers to this moment as "the tragedy of Gollum who at that moment came within a hair of repentance—but for one rough word from Sam" (*Letters*, 96). Gollum recoiled. The green glint flickered in his eyes and did not leave again. From that moment forward, Gollum wholeheartedly committed to his path—he led the hobbits into Shelob's tunnel to be killed. But his plans went crooked, and the hobbits survived.

Days later, Gollum found them scrambling up the Slopes of Doom. Gollum attacked Frodo in a final attempt for the Ring, but Frodo cast him away and continued toward his doom. In this moment, Sam had made up his mind to kill Gollum, but he wavered as understanding finally dawned on him. Gollum deserved death, Sam thought, and yet he was overcome by the same pity that had guided Frodo in his dealings with Gollum. "He himself, though only for a little while, had borne the Ring, and now dimly he guessed the agony of Gollum's shriveled mind and body, enslaved to that Ring, unable to find peace or relief ever in life again. But Sam had no words to express what he felt" (*LOTR*, Book VI, ch. 3). Sam had finally learned empathy for Gollum and so spared his life.

In our own lives, our experiences of suffering, loss, and grief can teach us how to be servants of mercy like Frodo and Sam. In this way, mercy can be an accompaniment to grief. To have mercy on others, to accept the mercy of others, to have mercy on oneself, is to soften the blows of grief and suffering.

Nienna, the Vala of Pity

The themes of mercy and pity are so deeply woven into Tolkien's story world that he built those qualities into the origins of his most important characters.

It is told in *The Silmarillion* that one of the Valar, Nienna, mourned for every wound that the world had suffered. She did not weep for herself but only for others, so her part in the music of the Ainur was one of lamentation.

Through her mourning, she was gifted with wisdom and understanding. She passed this wisdom down to any who would listen to her, teaching "pity, and endurance in hope . . . for she brings strength to the spirit and turns sorrow to wisdom" (*Silm*, Valaquenta). One of those who listened to her is named Olórin, wisest of all the Maiar. In the halls of Nienna, he learned pity and patience, which equipped him to help return the Children of Ilúvatar from despair and darkness. But you may know Olórin by another name: Gandalf. When all other wizards failed in their tasks, Gandalf remained steadfast because his heart was rooted in mercy.

In contrast to Nienna, Tolkien described Morgoth as being pitiless, writing in *The Silmarillion*, "To him that is pitiless the deeds of pity are ever strange and beyond reckoning" (*Silm*, ch. 24). In his pride, Morgoth did not account for the pity of the Valar upon the Children of Ilúvatar and instead believed they had abandoned Middle-earth into his power. As the "shadow of Morgoth," Sauron was similarly confounded by acts of mercy and pity—and this was his undoing.

The Story of Jonah

Few may be aware that Tolkien was credited as a principal collaborator on the Jerusalem Bible, an English translation of the Catholic Bible completed in the 1960s. His primary work for this project was in translating the Old Testament book of Jonah.

The story of Jonah is an account of a prophet running away from God's will for his life; God had instructed him to bring a message of repentance to the city of Ninevah, the land of his enemy, and instead of doing so, he fled. His rebellion causes a great storm, and he was ultimately cast into the sea. After being swallowed up by a great fish, Jonah finally repented and was then returned to land, where he did as God instructed. Upon hearing his message, the people of Ninevah immediately repented. Rather than respond with joy or gratitude at their conversion, however, Jonah was angered by God's mercy.

Tolkien felt that the real point of Jonah's story was "that God is much more merciful than 'prophets,' is easily moved by penitence, and won't be dictated to even by high ecclesiastics whom he has himself appointed" (*Letters*, 196a). Jonah's story reminds us that God desires mercy for everyone, even our enemies or the people we don't like.

Absolute Evil

Despite the evil deeds of Morgoth and Sauron, Tolkien explained in a letter that he did not believe in absolute evil: "In my story I do not deal in absolute evil. I do not think there is such a thing, since that is zero. I do not think that at any rate any 'rational being' is wholly evil. Satan fell" (*Letters*, 183). Elrond echoed this sentiment in the Council of Elrond when he stated, "For nothing is evil in the beginning. Even Sauron was not so" (*LOTR*, Book II, ch. 2).

When the world was created, it was good. For Tolkien, to be alive is to be part of this goodness. Evil is not an opposing force that exists separately from goodness, but instead it is a deprivation or distortion of goodness. Creation and life itself is inherently good, and any evil that exists is a deprivation or corruption of goodness.

Think of absolute good as 100 percent and absolute evil as 0 percent (which would then not exist as anything). Since being alive is good, nothing alive can equal 0 percent goodness. Actions can be 100 percent evil, but created beings can't. If no living being is absolutely evil, this means that no living being is beyond redemption. The extent to which a person has committed themselves to evil certainly erodes their own sense of goodness, and as such redemption would require a great deal of rehabilitation on their part. The point is that pity and mercy should direct all of our dealings with people because where there's life, there is hope. To be alive is to retain a degree of goodness.

Humphrey Carpenter's biography of Tolkien recounts a story of Tolkien offering a captured German soldier a drink of water, a testament to his belief that the men fighting on the other side of the war were still human and deserving of mercy. Tolkien also wrote in his letters that he felt the young men he was fighting against were no less brave or patriotic than the men fighting for England, and that the great loss of war was the reckless loss of human life (*Letters*, 45).

Tolkien learned mercy very tangibly during his experience of war, later drawing a distinction between an evil cause that may be pursued by the "other side" and the acts of heroism, sacrifice, and mercy of individual soldiers (*Letters*, 183). Through it all, he advocated for all judgments of others to be "tempered by 'mercy': that is, since we can with good will do this without the bias inevitable in judgements of ourselves, we must estimate the limits of another's strength and weigh this against the force of particular circumstances" (*Letters*, 246).

Ultimately, when the power of the Ring finally overcame Frodo's will, it was Gollum who brought about its destruction. There's a profound, poetic, and providential justice in how the creature most wretchedly enslaved by the Ring ultimately became the instrument of its demise and the world's deliverance. It's a reminder that Providence can work through the worst of us to bring about something beautiful and redemptive. We are reminded, in the glimpse of his humanity, that even Sméagol was created for goodness—and even though the power of the Ring had caused him to wander so far from his original path, Providence could still work through him to help heal the world.

Gollum carried the Ring for nearly five hundred years. And as he carried it, it carried *him* away from everything beautiful or kind or true he had ever known. When he took the Ring for himself, he entered into his own personal hell on earth—he was consumed by it until the final moment of his life. It was then that the wisdom of Gandalf was finally realized, and Frodo remarked to Sam, "But do you remember Gandalf's words: Even Gollum may have something yet to do? But for him, Sam, I could not have destroyed the Ring.

The Quest would have been in vain, even at the bitter end. So let us forgive him!" (*LOTR*, Book VI, ch. 3).

The story of Sméagol is one of great loss and tragedy. There are also so many parallels between his character and Frodo's that they can, in some ways, serve as narrative foils. Two hobbits, each receiving the Ring as they come of age, both led by it on journeys that brought them far away, both enemies and victims of the malice of Sauron, both unable to fully return home in the end. Often we might be tempted to look at others—maybe those living radically different lives than us, those who believe differently than us, those we disagree with—and see them as something less than human. We have to resist this temptation! Much like Sauron and Galadriel, Frodo and Sméagol illustrate the power of a person's choice to lead them in opposite directions. In the context of our own lives, the choices we make have led us all down our own paths, some deep into the tunnels of the Misty Mountains, some to the dungeons of Barad-Dur, some to the Field of Cormallen. But we're all a part of the same tale. By letting mercy guide our actions, we can leave room for Providence to act.

THE ROAD GOES ON

Reflect on your experience with mercy. What is a moving experience of mercy that shaped your life? In what ways might you be more merciful in your typical experiences each week? Consider visiting the Catholic Prison Ministry Coalition website for resources on ministering to those who are incarcerated: https://www.catholicprisonministries.org. You might also consider writing or calling your local representatives to advocate on behalf of those in most need.

Chapter 12

GROW THROUGH GRIEF

Values: Perseverance, Firmness, Resolution, and Conviction

> For a while they stood there, like men on the edge of a sleep where nightmare lurks, holding it off, though they know that they can only come to morning through the shadows.
>
> *LOTR*, Book IV, ch. 2

Two tired hobbits stand upon the edge of a broken cliff, gazing wearily down and across endless barren miles of the land of Shadow. What trees once grew here have turned to ash or been stripped barren. The memory of meadow and grass is now buried beneath layers upon layers of decay; the air is heavy with poison, smoke, and death. No bird or growing plant can be found for miles; neither the new life of spring nor the first-fruits of summer would ever come to this land again. To be in the land of Mordor was to abandon all life, to enter into hell. For Frodo and Sam, their path forward is shrouded in darkness, but they know that the only way to morning is through the shadow.

Grief is an inescapable aspect of life; to live is to experience suffering and loss alongside joy and new life. While some may experience more loss than others, no one escapes its touch. Everyone who lives will suffer, but how we respond to this suffering can shape us. To open one's heart to joy or life is to also open it to loss. This may sound scary, but the thought of living a life without joy or love is even scarier. There are certain risks to experiencing life wholeheartedly, but they are worth it. The alternative is to harden your heart, to close it off from both grief and joy. It would be easy to do so—comfortable even. But refusing to harden your heart can be both heroic and transformative.

Elrond Half-elven

Elrond Half-elven endured many lifetimes of grief. What could have made him bitter, resentful, or cold instead molded him into a gentle spirit, "as noble and as fair in face as an elf-lord, as strong as a warrior, as wise as a wizard, as venerable as a king of dwarves, and as kind as summer" (*The Hobbit*, ch. 3). How did he keep his heart soft in the midst of such loss? The lessons that we can learn from Elrond's life are manifold.

After the flight of his parents to the Blessed Realm, he and his twin brother, Elros, were left orphaned. Because of their parents, the half-elven brothers were given the chance to choose their own fate, to be counted among the elves or men. Elrond chose the immortality of the elves whereas his brother Elros chose the mortality of men. Eventually, as all men must, Elros died. And Elrond lived on.

Elrond later married Celebrían, the daughter of Galadriel, and together they had three children: twin sons Elladan and Elrohir and a daughter named Arwen. Their season of joy ended when Celebrían was captured and tormented by orcs. She was rescued by her sons and healed in body by Elrond, but she never recovered in spirit. Ultimately, she left Middle-earth to seek healing in the Blessed Realm.

Like Elrond and Elros, the children of Elrond were also given the choice between mortality and immortality. Elrond's daughter, Arwen, chose mortality, meaning that her fate would be forever separated from her father's.

Over his thousands of years of life, Elrond witnessed the growing power of darkness that loomed over Middle-earth. By the time Frodo arrived in Rivendell with Sauron's ring, Elrond had already perceived the suffering that lay ahead. Tolkien writes, "For Elrond, therefore, all chances of the War of the Ring were fraught with sorrow" (*LOTR*, appendix A).

Despite all doubt or cynicism, Elrond's resolution to remain hopeful was seen most clearly in his fostering of the young Aragorn, who was given the elvish name Estel ("Hope"). In preserving and safeguarding the descendants of Isildur, Elrond watered his hope for the future. He constantly strove against evil, never relenting or becoming bitter despite so many losses. For Elrond to remain as kind as summer was an act of resistance against evil; he was the embodiment of our scriptural command not to harden our hearts (Hebrews 4:7). In the context of our own lives, it is up to each of us to choose how we respond to suffering. Inspired by Elrond, we can choose to let our grief both strengthen our resolve and soften our hearts.

Frodo's Journey into Darkness

Frodo's quest plunged him headfirst into the darkest night any hobbit would ever know. Few of even the greatest heroes have endured Sauron's wrath directly, and none had ever sought to destroy the Ring and lived. In the end, Frodo fared better than anyone could've imagined. Yet he still did not return home unchanged; instead, Frodo was transformed—and bore a physical reminder of his journey by being pierced with a wound that would never heal.

Frodo's grace in bearing his own wounds and burdens brings me comfort because, like him, I have experienced griefs that will never leave me. It is also a powerful image of carrying grief for people or places we've lost because it reminds us that they will always stay with us. Through grief and remembrance, we carry the things we lose with us.

I have had two miscarriages: I will never know what the voices of those children would have sounded like, what their favorite colors would have been, or whether they'd look more like their dad or me. I have lost two of my grandparents: I will never know if they are proud of me for writing this book, or what they'd think of my life today. I have lost someone I dearly loved to suicide; in the years that have passed since their death, there have been so many times when I've wished I could tell them something, or ask them something, or share something with them.

I have struggled with bouts of depression, severe anxiety, and self-doubt for most of my life, and the imagery that Tolkien uses in connecting sunshine, stars, spring, and light with victory over grief has been surprisingly grounding and life-saving for me. If I can believe that the sun will rise again tomorrow, or that the stars are still shining even when I cannot see them, I can outlast the darkness.

In his lowest moment, Sam Gamgee sang, "Above all shadows rides the sun, and stars for ever dwell, I will not say the day is done nor bid the stars farewell" (*LOTR*, Book VI, ch. 1). I carry this song in my heart, and with it I have weathered many storms.

Not All Tears Are an Evil

But still, grief is not a thing to fear. Even as it signals to us our loss, it can serve as an anchor, a weighted blanket, or an invisible string connecting us to the things we've lost. Grief can be sacred and should be honored as a reflection of the measure of our love.

When Gandalf bade farewell to the hobbits at the Grey Havens, he recognized and empathized with their sorrow at his departure. He responded by saying, "Go in peace! I will not say: do not weep; for not all tears are an evil" (*LOTR*, Book VI, ch. 9). Gandalf acknowledged their pain and validated their tears. Even Jesus wept.

To experience loss can be isolating by its nature, because whatever has been lost is no longer present to us. There is no visible reminder or signal to others of the wound that pierces our heart. Instead, we are left with arms empty, chairs empty, milestones unmet, and anniversaries uncelebrated. We often carry these burdens alone. Grief makes people uncomfortable—they often don't know what to say;

they might be frightened by it; they might even forget it entirely. We shouldn't let that stop us from reaching out to share stories of those we've lost—it's in the sharing of stories that we better understand who they were for us.

If you know someone who has suffered a loss, mark the date in your calendar and reach out to them to simply let them know you remember. You don't have to be a grief counselor to recognize the burden someone might be carrying—acknowledging their pain itself is a great comfort because it helps them know they are not alone.

Symbols of Light and Darkness

Tolkien used many symbols of the natural world as heralds of victory. The natural world was a sign of goodness that evil continuously sought to mar—its consistent persistence is itself a sign of hope.

Frodo's story began in autumn, a time of growing darkness when the leaves are shed from their branches and blanket the earth in expectation of winter. He then passed through the "death" of winter, and his quest was finished in the first days of spring.

Overwhelmed by joy, Sam Gamgee remarked in the Field of Cormallen, "I feel like spring after winter, and sun on the leaves; and like trumpets and harps and all the songs I have ever heard!" (*LOTR*, Book VI, ch. 4). Spring represents or calls to mind images of hope, new life, a fresh start. It brings light after dark, warmth after the cold, cleansing rains, and gentleness after the harshness of winter. It is soft and joyful, a season to be celebrated.

Tolkien was a lover of myth and symbol and the natural rhythms of the seasons, and the way *The Lord of the Rings* flows is a testament to these sensibilities. Tolkien wrote about the setting for this story: "Seasons are carefully regarded. . . . The main action begins in autumn and passes through winter to a brilliant spring: this is basic to the purport and tone of the tale" (*Letters*, 210).

Similarly, Tolkien used the symbols of dark and light to signify the triumph of good over evil. When Arda was first made, it lay in a quiet darkness with only stars to light the sky. In this time, and throughout any times of darkness, we can remember that in the darkness of the night the stars shine more brightly. Eärendil's star was the clearest example of this.

Eventually, the sun and moon were made as a defense against Morgoth. When the sun was first created, Morgoth was confounded by its light. He attempted to make war against the sun itself but found it was beyond his reach. The orcs, servants of Morgoth and later Sauron, were unable to walk beneath the light of the sun. This story offers other examples of how the presence of the sun was a sign of hope for men, whereas the absence of sunlight was a sign of doom: When Minas Tirith was under siege, Gandalf told Pippin that there would be no dawn the following day because the forces of Sauron were nearly upon them; and in his wretchedness, Gollum hid himself from both the sun and moon.

Interestingly, Tolkien often equates hubris with darkness. Those who walk in the dark are unable to see, and those who would intentionally shroud themselves in darkness do so to their own detriment. Ultimately, Sauron was undone by his own devices as the shadow that he created to protect himself was used against him. Sam used the road that Sauron himself made to climb the slopes of Mount Doom; he and Frodo entered Mount Doom through the door that Sauron himself had also made. Tolkien wrote, "The Dark Lord was suddenly aware of him, and his eye piercing all shadows looked across the plain to the door that he had made; and the magnitude of his own folly was revealed to him in a blinding flash, and all the devices of his enemies were at last laid bare" (*LOTR*, Book VI, ch. 3).

The rhythm to the seasons consoles me when I'm wading through suffering or loss—it reminds me that life goes on and will bring new light. Spring brings new life, and each morning brings the rising sun. Nothing lasts forever, and that includes any shadow that darkens the sky at any given moment.

The Story of Job

In addition to his translation of Jonah, Tolkien also consulted on the translation of the book of Job for the Jerusalem Bible. The book of Job tells the story of a prosperous and devout man named Job whose faith is tested through suffering. As Job's life falls apart, he debates several of his friends—and then ultimately God himself—over the nature of suffering. Despite his confusion and frustration, Job never renounces God; as a reward for his faithfulness, his health and prosperity are restored at the end of the story.

The story offers lessons about compassion, perseverance, and faithfully enduring suffering. Job teaches us that while we may never fully understand the reasons for our sufferings in this life, we do not have to endure them alone. In a world that often depicts faith as sterile or serene, Job shows us what it looks like to authentically bring our whole heart to God in prayer; the God who made us desires closeness with us and welcomes our grief, anger, sorrow, and doubt. While the world is filled with beauty and order, it also contains evil and chaos; the existence of suffering cannot be fully understood by humanity, and God gently asks Job to trust in his plans even when it's difficult to do so. This story is also a lesson in compassion, reminding us to have sympathy for those who are suffering instead of assigning guilt or blame. Through Job's great loss and endurance of suffering, he is ultimately restored—a symbol of the joys of heaven.

Transformed by Grief

From his earliest years, death followed Tolkien like a shadow. By 1918, at the age of twenty-six, Tolkien had experienced enough death to last a lifetime. In the foreword to the second edition of *The Lord of the Rings*, he recounted, "One has indeed personally to come under the shadow of war to feel fully its oppression; but as the years go by it seems now often forgotten that to be caught in youth by 1914 was no less hideous an experience than to be involved in 1939 and the following years. By 1918 all but one of my close friends were dead."

His grief was later compounded by the Second World War, in which two of his sons served. After more than fifty years of marriage, Edith Tolkien passed away in 1971. Tolkien was greatly bereaved after her death, writing that he did not feel "quite 'real' or whole" anymore (*Letters*, 332).

Tolkien was able to capture grief so piercingly in his stories because of how thoroughly it permeated his life. After enduring so many losses throughout his life, he could have easily become bitter or jaded. He could have hardened his heart and closed it off forever. He could have stopped writing or pursuing his passions. Instead, he chose to pour out his heart into the pages of his Legendarium.

As much as it is inevitable, grief is also transformative. In the same way that the First World War would leave Tolkien changed forever, the wounds Frodo endured on his journey would also never leave him. We will all experience seasons of darkness in our lives. Sometimes, it is necessary to pass through that darkness in order to see the light more clearly. Sometimes, we will have to wait out the night, cherishing the memory of the sun until we can see its radiance rising once more. And sometimes that dawn won't happen in our lifetime—sometimes our problems can't be solved in this life. That's where the elven sense of *estel* comes in once again: We can cling to faith, knowing that we were created for goodness and are sustained within the plans of Providence. If we let it, this belief can be both an anchor and guiding light.

Tolkien's heroes did not avoid suffering. It was their endurance of this suffering without falling into despair that revealed their strength most clearly. Learning to live amidst both joy and sorrow will help us anchor ourselves to eternal hope. As the elf Gildor said to Frodo, "The world is indeed full of peril, and in it there are many dark places; but still there is much that is fair, and though in all lands love is now mingled with grief, it grows perhaps the greater" (*LOTR*, Book II, ch. 6). This doesn't make evil into good but instead folds all things together toward ultimate goodness.

For good or for ill, the sun will rise again tomorrow. Whether we rise alongside it can never be known, yet there is a profound comfort in the knowledge that the world carries on regardless. Each day, amidst grief, new life continues to sprout forth. Winter passes and spring blooms. In learning to endure grief with perseverance, we can grow through whatever storms life sends our way.

THE ROAD GOES ON

Reflect on the way that grief has touched your life. Find a tangible and concrete way to connect yourself to that grief and acknowledge it. A few possible suggestions: Visit the grave of a loved one, attend a funeral for someone in your church community, or pray for someone who has passed away. You could also do something intentional to acknowledge someone else's grief—reach out to someone who has suffered a loss and offer to drop off a meal, help them with errands, or simply spend time with them.

Chapter 13

Look for the Happy Ending

Values: Faith, Consolation, Purpose, and Unbrokenness

> "Yes," said Frodo. "But do you remember Gandalf's words: Even Gollum may have something yet to do? But for him, Sam, I could not have destroyed the Ring. The Quest would have been in vain, even at the bitter end. So let us forgive him! For the Quest is achieved, and now all is over. I am glad you are here with me. Here at the end of all things, Sam."
>
> *LOTR*, Book VI, ch. 3

As they climb across the broken land of Mordor, Frodo and Sam have cast aside almost everything. They have no weapons, no extra clothing, no food or water. They have saved nothing for their return journey because they no longer believe there will be one. Frodo began this quest with the intention of finishing it faithfully, and he now holds back nothing. But at the very last moment, Frodo realizes that he is unable to accomplish this task: The Ring has claimed him, as he now claims it for himself. And yet, by some miracle, all is not lost. And through no merit or strength of Frodo's own, the Ring is destroyed.

The way in which both Frodo and Middle-earth are saved reflects Tolkien's original concept of "eucatastrophe," the "good catastrophe" that leads to a surprising but happy ending. Tolkien believed that Christ's Resurrection was the greatest eucatastrophe; the ultimate destruction of the Ring despite Frodo's failure was the great eucatastrophe of Tolkien's Legendarium. Both of these unexpected, happy endings instill a sense of consolation in our hearts, which does not erase suffering, but does redeem it.

The Unexpected Happy Ending

Tolkien believed that consolation, the happy ending, was the highest function of a fairy-story. He called this story dynamic "eucatastrophe"—a happy ending that does not deny the existence of all the grief and pain that came before but instead redeems it. Eucatastrophe, Tolkien writes, "denies (in the face of much evidence, if you will) universal final defeat and insofar is *evangelium* [Latin for "good news"], giving a fleeting glimpse of joy, joy beyond the walls of the world, poignant as grief" ("On Fairy-Stories").

Eucatastrophe is intrinsically connected to Tolkien's belief in Christianity and his assertion that the Christian story is the story that makes sense of reality—it is the deepest, truest story we have. In his letters, he further explained: "Man the story-teller would have to be redeemed in a manner consonant with his nature: by a moving story" (*Letters*, 89). In this same letter, Tolkien wrote that he felt *The Lord of the Rings* had become a "story of worth" when he found himself experiencing this sense of eucatastrophe upon reading it. Stories that produce this form of joy are good for our souls: All small eucatastrophes of the secondary world of literature will, in the end, point us to and offer us glimpses of the Great Eucatastrophe—the final redemption by which God will save us.

In the end, Frodo was not able to fully resist the temptation of the Ring. And yet the quest was still accomplished! The lesson here is not that we need to somehow become more than we already are, but only that we need to try—and trust that God, who works for our good, will accomplish what we need.

Frodo's Complete Surrender

The moment Frodo agreed to take the Ring to Mordor was like a step into the darkness because he did not know what was ahead. This was also the case for Sam, as he knew even less than Frodo did about their quest. Each knew about the basic tenets of their task but couldn't know exactly how it would play out.

Frodo knew that he was chosen to carry the Ring, even if he didn't know which direction to walk; Sam simply knew that he needed to be with Frodo, and he remained faithful to that conviction. When Frodo was paralyzed by Shelob's sting, Sam had a moment of near despair when he believed Frodo had died. He knew that his quest was tied to Frodo and did not know how to carry on without him—yet he still took Frodo's burden upon himself and struggled on. Even after they were reunited, there came a time when Frodo was so weak that Sam was compelled to carry Frodo; despite not knowing which direction to walk, he struggled up the Slopes of Doom "having no guidance but the will to climb as high as might be before his strength gave out and his will broke" (*LOTR*, Book VI, ch. 3).

Even as their strength failed them, Tolkien writes that Frodo and Sam felt a sudden call in their darkest hour: "'Now, now, or it will be too late!' He braced himself and got up. Frodo also seemed to have felt the call. He struggled to his knees" (*LOTR*, Book VI, ch. 3). Who called Frodo and Sam? While Tolkien doesn't specify whether this call came from Eru himself, one of the Valar, or perhaps Galadriel, we can understand it as a moment of divine Providence urging them forward.

But despite their complete surrender to their tasks, the power of the Ring was inexorable. Frodo failed. Had the story ended there, it would have made for a bewildering ending—if that truly were the end. But it was not!

In hindsight, the story had been building to this moment all along, and Frodo's failure is its natural conclusion. Even when he was still in the Shire, Frodo was unable to cast the Ring into his own fireplace. How could he have possibly hoped to do otherwise after months of toil, starvation, and temptation? Why did Gandalf and Elrond send Frodo on this journey knowing that he would never be able to let go of the Ring when the time came? It was because their trust wasn't in Frodo but in something greater. Without a worldly hope, *amdir*, they held on to an otherworldly hope, *estel*.

From its very beginning, this was an impossible quest. And yet to attempt it was both necessary and sufficient. To work against evil is imperative, even when it seems impossible. In the end, Frodo's victory wasn't found in his own accomplishments but in his commitment to resisting evil with every ounce of his strength. Having the integrity to respond to evil with resistance allows Providence the room to work. As Tolkien explained in a letter, "Frodo had done what he could and spent himself completely (as an instrument of Providence) and had produced a situation in which the object of his quest could be achieved" (*Letters*, 246). In our own lives, we never know how far our seemingly small efforts will go in God's hands.

Weighed down by grief and yet not having fully succumbed to despair, Frodo and Sam trudged toward the light with their last ounce of strength and will. And in the end, it was enough—not because of any power they themselves possessed, but because of Providence. We admire Frodo because of his complete surrender and commitment to his task, despite the unknowable outcome. Tolkien's genius is in characterizing the interplay between divine Providence and our inadequate efforts. We must do what we can, but our only hope is placing our trust in God.

Many people scoff at Frodo's failure, as if to say, "Sorry to Frodo, but I'm built different. I wouldn't have taken the Ring. Surely, I would resist temptation with complete success." But this false confidence misses the point of the story entirely. None of us are strong enough to stand up against the full might of evil—not on our own. Though Bilbo, Frodo, and Sam showed incredible resilience to the Ring, none of them were impervious. Even Tom Bombadil would have ultimately fallen before the full might of Sauron (*LOTR*, Book II, ch. 2). With the Ring, both Galadriel and Gandalf knew that they would have become even worse tyrants than Sauron himself.

Tolkien was surprised that some readers judged Frodo harshly, and responded to one such critic by writing,

> Frodo deserved all honor because he spent every drop of his power of will and body, and that was just sufficient to bring him to the destined point, and no further. Few others, possibly no others of his time, would have got so far. The Other Power then took over: the writer of the story (by which I do not mean myself), "that one ever-present Person who is never absent and never named." (*Letters*, 192)

Providence had guided Frodo for months upon tireless months, and it did not abandon him in the very end. Frodo's submission to the power of the Ring was short-lived, and ultimately Sauron fell despite his momentary victory. Because of all of his previous work in resisting its temptation, Frodo created the perfect conditions for Providence to redeem his "failure."

Tolkien was familiar with the many short-term victories of evil, echoing this sentiment in a 1944 letter to his son Christopher: "All we do know, and that to a large extent by direct experience, is that evil labors with vast power and perpetual success—in vain: preparing always only the soil for unexpected good to sprout in" (*Letters*, 64). Tolkien's trust in Providence and faithfulness gave him a strong sense of being rooted in an ultimate victory despite facing many inevitable defeats along the way. He didn't believe that the result would ever be lacking, but instead that the result would actually be made more beautiful as these defeats were woven into the ultimate plan in a mysterious way.

St. Mary Magdalene, Witness to the Resurrection

To be faithful is to remain true to one's convictions and purpose, to remain steadfast and loyal, to withstand temptation and doubt until the very end. Conversely, to be called "faithless" is terrible; Gandalf calls Sauron "faithless and accursed" (*LOTR*, Book V, ch. 10).

If we believe in the concept of Providence or Fate, we can begin to see a world held together by a power who works toward goodness, somehow *through* our free will. And that is an encouraging thought.

Everyone is called to do something with their lives; we were each created with a purpose. When Providence makes itself apparent, our task is to chase after it with as much perseverance and commitment as we can.

St. Mary Magdalene is a great example of faithfulness, and her witness to Christ's Resurrection was a powerful consolation. Called the "Apostle to the Apostles" by St. Thomas Aquinas, Mary faithfully followed Christ through his ministry and tribulations. Along with several other women, Mary Magdalene accompanied Jesus as he carried his Cross to Golgotha and then remained at the foot of the Cross until after his death.

When most of Christ's disciples abandoned him, Mary remained faithful through these dark hours. Her faithfulness was later rewarded when she found Christ's tomb empty, making her the first witness to the greatest eucatastrophe of all time. Mary Magdalene is recognized as one of the greatest female saints and biblical figures, and her faithfulness can be a powerful example for each of us.

Good Brought Out of Evil

Just as Christ's death brought about new life, there are many ways in which evil is folded into the plans of goodness—this is true in Tolkien's myth as well as in our own lives. During the creation of Tolkien's world, the discord of Morgoth arose and disrupted the harmony of creation. In response, Eru allowed creation to continue on despite the fact that it departed from his original plan. Instead of Morgoth's actions working against Eru, his evil was instead folded into the plans of Eru. Through his alterations, the world was made more wonderful than previously imagined.

Tolkien believed that Providence worked all things toward an ultimate good, a belief translated into his mythology through Eru's response to Morgoth's rebellion. After the music of the Ainur had ceased, Eru spoke to Morgoth, saying, "And thou, [Morgoth], shalt see that no theme may be played that hath not its uttermost source in me, nor can any alter the music in my despite. For he that attempteth this shall prove but mine instrument in the devising of things more wonderful, which he himself hath not imagined" (*Silm*, Ainulindalë).

Tolkien illustrated this mystery brilliantly with an example of water. During his rebellion, Morgoth created extreme heat and cold that had not been originally intended. Because of these changes, however, water was transformed into snow, rain, frost, and mist. While the deeds of Morgoth still remained evil, they brought about a new form of beauty because they were woven into the will of Eru. While evil still remains evil, faith holds that Providence will transform the works of evil in pursuit of an ultimate good.

Ultimately, Sauron was defeated through each character's faithful commitment to their purpose. Gandalf was sent to Middle-earth for a very specific purpose, and he remained until Sauron had been utterly defeated. Aragorn was meant to ascend to the throne of Gondor, and he did so after the War of the Ring had ended. Bilbo was meant to find the Ring, and he passed it on to Frodo, who was meant to carry it—and he carried it with all of his strength. Other characters may have less obvious fates, but in following their convictions, they each brought the story that much closer to its consolation.

THE ROAD GOES ON

Make a habit of looking for the consolations in your own daily life, the small eucatastrophes that come your way. Noting these victories, and relishing them, will bring hope when things seem dark. Consider keeping a journal or list to write down these moments as they happen, and reread it when you need encouragement.

Chapter 14

LET GO OF YOUR "RING"

Values: Temperance, Sacrifice, Altruism, and Detachment

> I tried to save the Shire, and it has been saved, but not for me. It must often be so, Sam, when things are in danger: some one has to give them up, lose them, so that others may keep them. But you are my heir: all that I had and might have had I leave to you.
>
> *LOTR*, Book VI, ch. 9

The years following the destruction of the Ring are beautiful. New life is bursting forth from the Shire as the shadow of Sauron begins to fade from memory. The harvests are abundant, and new children are born. For Merry and Pippin and Sam, these years have brought the beginnings of a full and abundant life. But for Frodo, there is no coming home. The Morgul-wound pains him, and he is haunted by the memory of the Ring. Ultimately, Frodo realizes that the Shire had been saved, but not for him.

As we come to the end of our journey together, we will examine the theme of sacrifice in *The Lord of the Rings* and reflect on the way that it is sometimes necessary for us to lose something in order to save it. We will also reflect on what happens when a person is unable to let go of something "precious" even when it is destroying them.

Letting Go of the Ring

As the song and dance of his eleventy-first birthday celebration carried on across the hill despite his mysterious disappearance, Bilbo Baggins wavered on the threshold of Bag End with a decision to make. The air was still as if the world itself held its breath, because something was happening that had never happened in all its history: The One Ring would be given up freely.

A thing of great beauty, this Ring had worn its way into the heart of this hobbit for more than fifty years. But adventure called once more, and this time Bilbo would leave his treasure behind to pursue it. He felt thin, stretched, and in need of a change. And so he would accomplish something even the great kings of old were unable to do as he passed on this precious Ring to his heir and nephew, Frodo. Though he didn't know it, this simple act of surrender would set the tone for Frodo's own journey. Immediately after giving up the Ring, Bilbo was washed over with a sense of peace, and he laughed in relief. With a newfound sense of freedom and lightheartedness, Bilbo allowed himself to be swept onto the road again for one last adventure. "I'm as happy now as I've ever been," he remarked to Gandalf (*LOTR*, Book I, ch. 1).

The manner in which a person received the One Ring was crucial to understanding its effect on them. Unlike Gollum, who gained the Ring for himself through murder and deceit, Bilbo had found it by accident and allowed pity to guide his interactions with Gollum. In the same way, Frodo inherited the Ring lawfully and without self-interest or guilt. Both Bilbo and Frodo were able to resist the Ring's corruption for as long as they did, in part, because of the way they received the Ring—they did not seek it out.

Bilbo's sacrifice in giving up the Ring was a gift both to himself and to Frodo, and Frodo would imitate this sacrifice in his own experience of carrying the Ring. His ultimate journey to the Blessed Realm was the culmination of the decision he had made long before. Frodo had already made the decision to "lose" the Shire for himself way back in the first chapters of *The Fellowship of the Ring*, but now that decision is finally put into action. He never intended to wield the Ring for himself. Upon learning of its power, his immediate response was to hide it or to offer it to Gandalf who might destroy it. He took the Ring on his quest as a steward and not a master of it—at least until the very last moment when the Ring claimed him. Even though he ultimately yielded to the power of the Ring, it was his intent and the fact that he gave his entire self for the quest that is important.

Frodo's journey was driven by his love for the Shire. Even before he took his first steps away from home, he knew that he would likely never return, and yet he carried on anyway. As each step brought him farther from home, he was one step closer to saving the Shire for those he loved. It was a journey of continually surrendering and letting go.

Ultimately because of Frodo's sacrifice, the Shire was saved. But his journey changed him so profoundly that he was unable to return to the life he knew before. In the end, Frodo had to lose the Shire in order to save it.

It might seem baffling or like folly to some, but Frodo's actions are reminiscent of Christ's sacrifice in the deep story of reality that Tolkien perceived through faith. Similarly, Eärendil also makes a monumental sacrifice for the good of others. Though he succeeded in petitioning the Valar for aid in the defeat of Morgoth, he was unable to return home afterward. In their self-sacrifice, both Eärendil and Frodo embodied the words of the Gospel: "If any want to become my followers, let them deny themselves and take up their cross and follow me" (Matthew 16:24). Through this sacrifice comes new life, as exemplified by Christ's Resurrection and redemption of humanity. Through our own sacrifices, we participate in this same divine mystery of new life and grow in our capacity to care for one another more fully, pursue goodness even when it's uncomfortable or inconvenient, and experience renewed energy and peace in the midst of giving ourselves away.

St. Bernadette and Frodo

Bernadette Soubirous was born in 1844 in the town of Lourdes in southern France. Her family lived in poverty, and she suffered from poor health. One day, while gathering firewood for her family, Bernadette was met by a vision of a beautiful woman in a grotto. This was the first of her many visions of Mary.

In one of her visions, the woman instructed Bernadette to dig a well; from this hole came a spring of clear water. As the news of her visions spread, thousands of people began to flock to these waters to experience miraculous healings. Bernadette, however, never sought out her own healing; instead, she passed away in 1879 at the age of thirty-five.

In January 1945, Tolkien and his wife, Edith, went to the cinema to see a film about St. Bernadette. He was deeply moved by this story, as evident by his references to it in several letters in the months following. An interest and devotion to St. Bernadette continued for the rest of his life.

In a letter from 1954, Tolkien explained that the essence of *The Lord of the Rings* could be found in the parallel between Frodo and St. Bernadette:

> For me the "kernel" is in Frodo's last words to Sam: "I have been too deeply hurt. I tried to save the Shire, and it has been saved, but not for me. It must often be so, Sam, when things are in danger: someone has to give them up, lose them, so that others may keep them . . . all that I had or might have had, I leave to you." Bernadette refused to go to Lourdes for her own healing. (*Letters*, 148a)

St. Bernadette suffered from sickness her entire life, but she would not receive healing. Instead, she waited patiently until her time came to pass out of this world and into heaven. In Frodo, we can see an image of St. Bernadette—he was unable to recover from his wounds within Middle-earth and had to pass into the Blessed Realm to receive healing. It might seem odd that Bernadette didn't seek out her own healing—and she wouldn't have been wrong to do so—but she chose to place her trust in the eternal and anchor her hope in a life beyond this one. In doing so, she took up a heroic sacrifice.

One of the greatest tragedies of *The Lord of the Rings* is the fact that Frodo is unable to return to his ordinary hobbit life after the Ring's destruction. On his return journey to the Shire, Gandalf warned Frodo that there are some wounds that cannot be wholly healed. Frodo recognized that for him, there was no real return: "Though I may come to the Shire, it will not seem the same; for I shall not be the same" (*LOTR*, Book VI, ch. 7).

Tolkien explained, "His real desire was hobbitlike (and humanlike) just 'to be himself' again and get back to the old familiar life that had been interrupted" (*Letters*, 246). Frodo had actually expected to die to fulfill his quest, and so he didn't quite know how to process the fact that he survived. Because of how profoundly his journey had changed him, he was unable to pick up his old life. But because of his role in the Ring's destruction, Frodo was granted a place of healing and contemplation before his death.

The Corruption of Self-Centeredness

While we admire the courageous self-sacrifice of Tolkien's heroes, we can also learn from the cautionary tales of those who fell to the allure of the Ring. As Sauron rose to power in the Second Age, nine rings were given to the race of men, who "proved easier to ensnare" than elves or dwarves; through the power of the rings they "obtained glory and great wealth, yet it turned to their undoing" (*Silm*, Of the Rings of Power and the Third Age). Like Sauron, we can imagine that these men began with fair motives: They may have sought to use these rings to protect or defend their people, to claim an authority they felt entitled to, or to bring stability through wealth. Through his power, Sauron sought to subvert the order of life: Whereas Providence wove all things toward an ultimate good, even the best intentions were turned to evil in Sauron's hands. In their alliance with Sauron, these men ultimately became his slaves; they were called the Nazgûl, the Ringwraiths.

This process did not happen immediately. Instead, Sauron's power corrupted them slowly, each according to his disposition, meaning that each of these men could have renounced Sauron before it was too late—but they chose not to. Maybe they grew too comfortable, maybe they were afraid, maybe they enjoyed the power Sauron's work afforded them; ultimately, their refusal to let go of their rings was their downfall. Rather than resisting the dark lord, they accepted both his gifts and his terms and ultimately lost themselves in the process.

In a similar way, we can see this same corrupting power at work through the One Ring as it gnawed at the hearts of any who came near it: It was *precious*, it was *admirable*, it would be *folly* to cast it away. Like the Nazgûl, the fates of both Isildur and Boromir are tragic reminders of Sauron's duplicity. While they are often mischaracterized as villains or antagonists, they can be more fittingly seen as representations of the everyman. Both valiant and courageous heroes, Isildur and Boromir were drawn to the Ring through fair motives but were ultimately betrayed. Had either of these men resisted the Ring's promises, their stories would have ended much differently. Instead, evil was allowed to endure for a while longer.

We often witness the consequences of a person being unwilling to relinquish power, status, or pleasure—even when it is destroying them. We might recognize this temptation as a struggle within our own hearts, in someone we love, or in the life of a public figure—it is a slow-changing corruption that can be eerily similar to Tolkien's description of men becoming wraiths who "had, as it seemed, unending life, yet life became unendurable to them" (*Silm*, Of the Rings of Power and the Third Age). We see this all the time when political leaders abandon their principles in pursuit of advancement or reelection. With the advent of social media, influencers often promote trends that bring clout but damage health and integrity. In our own lives, we likely recognize the toll that some choices, habits, or lifestyles are taking on us: These are the things that leave us feeling "thin, sort of stretched, if you know what I mean: like butter that has been scraped over too much bread" (*LOTR*, Book I, ch. 1). In learning to let go of these things, we will find our hearts lighter and our journeys easier.

The Mystery of Sacrifice and New Life

Tolkien was keenly aware of the sacrifices that sometimes must be made to protect home or family. He saw his mother as a martyr for her faith, sacrificing her own health for the sake of raising her sons in a faith tradition she believed to be true. He also experienced this sacrifice very tangibly in the case of war, in which a soldier must leave their own home in order to defend it.

I have tried to make a habit of welcoming opportunities for self-sacrifice. In my own experience, sometimes I have had to decline opportunities so that others could have them. As a parent, often I need to sacrifice my own time or comfort in order to care for my children. I maintain digital communications for a group of cloistered nuns in my town, filtering out genuine inquiries from the spam and hateful emails they receive so that they don't have to read them. I have taken over leadership of my church's annual festival when no other volunteers could be found; though I am happy to help, planning and running the event each year means that I don't get to enjoy it in the same way a participant would. While pulling weeds in my own yard, I'll spend a few minutes pulling the weeds in my elderly neighbor's yard as well. These are all small examples, and not meant to be self-congratulatory, but I share them here simply to show how this mindset can be applied practically. There are a million small ways that we can follow Frodo's example of sacrifice. We can sacrifice our own time so that others might save time of their own; we can go without something so another may have it; we can pass on an opportunity in order for another to receive it. When rooted in love, small sacrifices like these can lead to new and abundant life.

In other situations, sacrifice might mean letting go of something that we are holding onto that is ultimately keeping us back from our own vocation, goals, dreams, or needs. Like Frodo and Sam casting off their extra baggage and belongings and crawling up the slopes of Mount Doom, we should strive to cast aside anything that is hindering our own spiritual or interior life, such as unhealthy habits, distractions that waste time, compulsions, or destructive beliefs.

It helps to start out toward our goals with simple, small steps. Frodo began his journey when he was still in the Shire; he wasn't teleported straight to Mordor. If your goal is to run a marathon, you might begin by running a mile at a time. If you want to volunteer at a food bank, sign yourself up for one shift. If you struggle with any harmful habits, begin by replacing them with positive ones. Be gentle and generous with yourself, and take things slowly, keeping your goals in mind—trust that these small, daily choices will carry you much further than any immediate quick fixes might promise to.

Temperance is the virtue that brings balance and helps us set boundaries in our desires so we can pursue something greater. It is the virtue that shapes heroes, prompting them to self-denial for the sake of their ultimate goals. Temperance is antithetical to selfishness and domination—it frees us to follow the guiding star of our values and to let go of the things that hinder us in our growth or purpose.

One of life's most difficult lessons is that sometimes we must be willing to lose something in order to save it for another. This kind of self-sacrifice is love in action, and it is heroic. As we come toward the end of our journey together in this book, look back on the earliest chapters that focused on the "smallness" of Tolkien's heroes. We have walked alongside them for many miles to see how they have passed through fire. Through self-sacrifice, they have emerged refined. It can be the same for us, too.

THE ROAD GOES ON

What sacrifices are you called to make to support the people you love? What are the most challenging sacrifices—and how do they lead to new life? Take another step and reflect on the habits, belongings, or beliefs you might need to let go of in order to fully become the person you were made to be. What are your deepest desires, and what is holding you back from them? Create a few goals that can propel you to take some first steps toward that destination this week.

Epilogue

You Are Inside a Very Great Story!

"Why, to think of it, we're in the same tale still! It's going on. Don't the great tales never end?" "No, they never end as tales," said Frodo. "But the people in them come, and go when their part's ended. Our part will end later—or sooner."

LOTR, Book IV, ch. 8

We were brought together by a "great story" of the kind Frodo describes. In reading Tolkien, we enter into a great story, and if we open ourselves to it, we can return home changed. In a similar way, we can look at history as being one great story in which we play a small part. In May 1944, Tolkien wrote to his son Christopher, "Keep up your hobbitry in heart, and think that all stories feel like that when you are in them. You are inside a very great story!" (*Letters*, 66).

Tolkien viewed God as the supreme storyteller who redeemed humanity through a compelling and moving story: the Gospel. He spoke of this story as the one in which all other stories have their roots. To view history as one great story can be grounding and heartening because we can learn from those who came before us and live our lives in a way that will benefit those who come after us.

And if this story has a divine author, then we can trust that each chapter of our lives is being written with intention to bring us to abundant life. If Tolkien's Legendarium was crafted with so much care and intention, we can trust that our own world, written by a divine author, is infinitely more so.

All of Our Stories Are Connected

In the same way that all of the great tales of Tolkien's Legendarium are connected through various stories and threads, we may see ourselves as being like hobbits who play a small part in a similarly large narrative. This concept feels abstract but can become more concrete when we learn more about our own histories. What did life look like for your grandparents, great-grandparents, or even great-great-grandparents? What were their passions, their dreams, their hopes?

Sometimes I'll look at old photographs of my great-grandparents and see features of my own face in theirs. Then I'll look down at my own children and see those same features in them, and I'll know that I'm a part of a great story. This same connection can also be felt tangibly when we read classic literature. In doing so, we realize that people who lived hundreds or even thousands of years before us have experienced many of the same joys, sorrows, problems, and feelings that we do now. We find a point of connection—a fellowship—that crosses space and time.

Elrond as a Bridge Between Ages

Elrond's history stretches far back into the elder days, from the First Age all the way into the Fourth Age. His presence in all three of the major works of the Legendarium allows him to serve as a bridge, connecting all of the ages of Middle-earth together.

To trace Elrond's family tree is to follow a thread through all of the ages of Arda: His foremother Melian the Maia was among the Ainur, more ancient than the earth itself. She was wed to Thingol, one of the first-born elves, and from their union came Lúthien. Lúthien married Beren, a man, and their son Dior was wed to

Nimloth. Their daughter Elwing wed Eärendil, and their sons were Elrond and his twin brother Elros, who would grow to become the first king of Númenor. As the ages of the world waned on, the line of Elros would continue even after the downfall of Númenor. The star of Eärendil that shone in the heavens was also a sign of this connection between the ages, along with the phial of Galadriel, which carried the star's light. Through the star, the story lives on. Just as Elrond's lineage can be traced back throughout the ages, we can see ourselves as being connected to the history of our own world. While our lives may feel short, they are but one part of a great story that will continue to unfold long after we are gone.

As Frodo said goodbye to Sam at the Grey Havens, he explained that he had left the last few pages of the book for him to fill. Cleverly, Tolkien also devoted the last few pages of *The Lord of the Rings* to detailing Sam's return home. By ending the story at Bag End, now transformed, Tolkien underscores the effect of Frodo's sacrifice. Because of Frodo, Sam has a home to return to. And his story would continue on for many years to come.

One Tree, Many Leaves

Just as each person is unique and irreplaceable, so too are stories. Tolkien wrote about stories as if there were one great tree from which all stories grew like leaves. They were all connected and originated from the same roots, but the branches pointed this way and that, and each leaf was unique in its own way. Each leaf tells a different story, speaking to different places within the history of the great tree. For Tolkien, all myth and story originated from the same source, but each one contains a different perspective and value. He believed that "all tales may come true; and yet, at the last, redeemed, they may be as like and as unlike the forms that we give them as man, finally redeemed, will be like and unlike the fallen that we know" ("On Fairy-Stories"). In the same way, we are each a unique and irreplaceable "leaf" in the great story of our world's history. Never forget that!

Toward the end of his reunion with Frodo in Rivendell, Bilbo sang softly to himself, "I sit beside the fire and think of all that I have seen, of meadow-flowers and butterflies in summers that have been" (*LOTR*, Book II, ch. 3). Age had begun to take a toll on him, and he reflected on the years of his life. In this moment with Frodo, he understood that the burden of the Ring and its story had now also passed on to Frodo. "Don't adventures ever have an end?" he asks. "I suppose not. Someone else always has to carry on the story" (*LOTR*, Book II, ch. 1).

Bilbo's song was a reflection on the passage of time over generations as he himself contemplated his own mortality. In many ways, his story speaks to a sense of being but a small part in the grand history of the world. There is a temptation to live our lives as if we are the "main character," as if all other stories are mere subplots to our own. Instead, Tolkien teaches us that we are but one part of a very grand story that spans thousands upon thousands of years and is much more important than whatever meaning we might cling to ourselves. There are millions of people who have lived before us, and there are many whose lives will begin after ours have ended. The span of our lives is but a small piece within the history of our world; it is our task to use our own lifetime to resist evil and defend goodness.

Farewell

As the hobbits prepared to return to the Shire after the War of the Ring had finally ended, they were distraught to realize that Gandalf did not intend to accompany them all the way home. They had come to rely on him, trusting in his guidance to lead them. But Gandalf knew that they were ready; their journeys had changed them, and they were ready to finish this final stretch without him. Like Gandalf, this is where I leave you. Now that we have walked this far together, it is time for you to discern your next steps.

To be a hobbit at heart has nothing to do with whether or not you like mushrooms, or dress in bright colors, or know how to garden or cook or host a party. It is about being rooted in your values, steadfast and courageous and faithful. If we are to live like a hobbit, we should strive to cherish the seasons of tender joy in our lives by slowing down, quieting our hearts and minds, and steeping ourselves in the goodness that surrounds us. Go seek out what is wholesome and beautiful in your life and rest in it. Nurture a life that supports your values and brings you peace. At the same time, we cannot forget that we are also called to look outside ourselves: A life well lived is an adventure of sacrifice, discomfort, and change. So while we are preparing our hearts by nourishing them, we cannot forget what we are preparing them for.

Much like Tolkien's hobbits, we must hold fast to our courage and step out onto the road ahead to meet whatever adventure awaits us. We must choose to set out on this adventure with Providence every day—it is not a once-and-for-all decision. This is a comforting reminder because none of us is perfect; so whenever we step off the path or wander astray, we can always find the way again. We have entered into Middle-earth together and now return home changed, carrying a part of it with us as we go out to make our own world a better place.

Since Tolkien's death, the love for Middle-earth has only grown throughout the world. His stories have inspired countless readers, planting the seeds of truth, beauty, and goodness in their hearts as they read. May we all be encouraged by his life, his work, and his faith to set out upon our own adventures with the same devotion, humility, and courage as the peoples of Middle-earth. I hope this book will sit on your shelf and be something that you can come back to someday when you need it again. Until then, "May the Shire live for ever unwithered!" (*LOTR*, Book V, ch. 8).

Namárië.

Acknowledgments

Thank you to my husband and our children for supporting me on this journey. Thank you to my editor, Josh Noem, for reaching out and suggesting I write this book and helping along every step of the way. Thank you to J. R. R. Tolkien for writing these stories that continue to inspire me to this day, and to his son Christopher for his heroic dedication and stewardship of Middle-earth after his father's death. Thank you to all of the friends who made themselves available for questions, brainstorming, proofreading, and editing: Marlene, Kiki, Gideon, Matt, Joe, Ken, Sarah, Zoe, Zac, Dawn, Erin, Fr. Mike, Jared, Brenna, Therese, and Kirk. Thank you to every member of the Tea with Tolkien community.

Appendix A

TOLKIEN'S STORY WORLD

Tolkien's Universe

The basic cosmology of Tolkien's world as presented in *The Silmarillion* is foundational to a discussion of the themes of *The Lord of the Rings*—here's a short summary.

In Tolkien's story, there is one supreme deity called Eru Ilúvatar, or the One, who existed before all other beings. In the beginning, Ilúvatar created the Ainur, angelic beings, and instructed them in divine music. Through the music of the Ainur, the world was created. The world was named Eä, or Arda. Some of these angelic beings came to dwell within the world and prepare it for the coming of its inhabitants, the Children of Ilúvatar. These angelic beings are divided into two "classes": The Valar are the governing beings, sometimes called gods (which can be likened to the gods of ancient mythology); along with them came the Maiar, who were of a lesser stature and often servants of the Valar. The Valar were more involved in the events of *The Silmarillion* but are still referenced in *The Lord of the Rings*. For example, Elbereth, Morgoth, Manwë, Aulë, and Oromë are named. Several of the Maiar played a prominent role in *The Lord of the Rings*, including Sauron, Gandalf, Saruman, and Balrogs.

The Children of Ilúvatar were the peoples of Middle-earth: elves, men (and women), hobbits, and ultimately dwarves. Each of these races was distinctly different, though hobbits belonged to the same classification as "men." The lifespan of elves was tied to the life of the earth, so they were essentially immortal; if their spirits were separated from their bodies, they would enter the Halls of Awaiting until they were re-embodied in the Blessed Realm. Humans and dwarves were mortal, and their fate after death is left unexplained in Tolkien's works.

The history of Arda was measured in ages, each spanning several thousands of years. Middle-earth was one continent within Arda. At the end of the First Age, a large portion of this continent, called Beleriand, was drowned. Aman, also called the Blessed Realm, was a continent located in the far west of Middle-earth; Valinor was the region of the Blessed Realm wherein the Valar and elves dwelt.

In the beginning, Arda was flat. At the end of the Second Age, it was reshaped into a globe. In this reshaping, the Blessed Realm was removed physically from the earth and remained accessible only to the elves, who reach it via a hidden path.

Tolkien's Stories

Here are some short summaries of a few of Tolkien's major works. For parents and teachers, I've also included what I think are good ages to introduce children to each book.

Tolkien referred to the collection of his writings, or myths, concerning Arda as his "Legendarium." Within this Legendarium, three books are discussed primarily: *The Hobbit*, *The Lord of the Rings*, and *The Silmarillion*. Please note that this section contains spoilers for major plot elements of these works.

The Hobbit

Published in 1937, *The Hobbit* follows the unexpected journey of an unassuming hobbit named Bilbo Baggins as he is whisked away from his comfortable and cozy home into a world of adventure by Gandalf the wizard and a company of thirteen dwarves. Along this journey, he will find many things: friendship, courage, and a small, magical ring that will forever change the course of his life.

When approaching Tolkien's Legendarium for the first time, *The Hobbit* is an excellent place to begin for readers young and old; depending on the sensitivity of your child, they may be ready to hear *The Hobbit* read aloud between ages five and eight.

The Lord of the Rings

After the widespread success of *The Hobbit*, a sequel was requested by Tolkien's publishers. In the summer of 1954, *The Fellowship of the Ring* was finally published, the first of three volumes that comprise *The Lord of the Rings. The Two Towers* and *The Return of the King* followed soon after.

Whereas Bilbo's adventure in *The Hobbit* saw this magical ring's arrival in Hobbiton, *The Lord of the Rings* would follow the journey of Bilbo's nephew, Frodo Baggins, who had inherited Bilbo's Ring. As the Ring is revealed to be the greatest weapon of the dark lord Sauron, Frodo will embark on a life-changing quest to cast it into the fires of Mount Doom.

The Lord of the Rings is a more dangerous and difficult read when compared to *The Hobbit,* though still quite manageable for most readers aged ten and up.

The Silmarillion

As published, *The Silmarillion* contains five major sections: "Ainulindalë," "Valaquenta," "The Quenta Silmarillion," "Akallabêth," and "Of the Rings of Power and the Third Age." The first three of these sections tell the story of the creation of the world and its earliest days, the First and Second Ages of Arda. Though these events occur first chronologically speaking, I don't recommend *The Silmarillion* as a starting point for new readers because of its breadth. The primary plot revolves around three jewels called the Silmarils. Created by the elven-smith Fëanor, these jewels contained the light of the Two Trees of Valinor and were themselves blessed. After the theft of these jewels by the primary villain Morgoth, Fëanor and his sons swore an oath to reclaim the Silmarils at any cost, forsaking Valinor and pursuing him across the sea to Middle-earth. The oath would result in a long and hopeless war lasting for centuries, until the Silmarils were ultimately lost forever. At the end of the First Age, Morgoth was defeated and thrust into the void.

"Akallabêth" recounts the story of the Second Age of Arda. After the defeat of Morgoth, the men who aided the elves and Valar in his defeat were rewarded with the island kingdom of Númenor. Númenor's first king was Elros, the twin brother of Elrond. The people of Númenor were granted a longer lifespan than other humans but were still mortal. In time, they began to resent the elves for their immortality and ultimately made war against the Blessed Realm in an attempt to claim immortality for themselves. Because of this rebellion, Ilúvatar removed the Blessed Realm from the earth, violently reshaping its geography. This resulted in an inescapable wave that destroyed Númenor. Those who escaped the downfall of Númenor fled to Middle-earth, where they founded the kingdoms of Gondor and Arnor.

In this time period, Morgoth's most powerful servant, Sauron, stepped into the role of primary villain. Whereas the First Age was primarily concerned with jewels, the Second Age was concerned with rings. Sauron seduced the peoples of Middle-earth and Númenor to his will, at first through subtlety but then through the power of the rings. Three rings were forged for the elves, seven for the dwarves, nine for men, and one for Sauron himself. At the end of the Second Age, the Last Alliance of elves and men resisted Sauron, and the Ring was cut from Sauron's finger. He was defeated, but only for a time.

"Of the Rings of Power and the Third Age" briefly tells the story of the Third Age, a narrative largely explored in *The Hobbit* and *The Lord of the Rings.*

While not explicit or graphic, *The Silmarillion* contains some intense and adult themes such as torture, incest (albeit accidental), and kinslaying. I would recommend waiting until children are thirteen before introducing *The Silmarillion.*

Appendix B

Interpretive Keys to Tolkien's Writing

In this book, we explore many of the values and ideas that bind *The Lord of the Rings* together and speak to the heart of Tolkien's story. Here are ten primary themes and three major principles that run through Tolkien's writing.

Ten Key Themes

- **Good and evil:** At its most basic level, *The Lord of the Rings* tells the story of the struggle of good against evil. Evil was represented first by Morgoth, followed later by his servant Sauron. Alliances were made between the different peoples of Middle-earth to resist Sauron, and good triumphed in the end.

- **Providence:** Throughout Frodo's quest there was "something else at work" in the story, an unseen force that opposed the will of Sauron (*LOTR*, Book I, ch. 2). This force was given many names: Fate, chance, doom, or luck; in his personal correspondence, Tolkien called it Providence (*Letters*, 246). While free will remained, characters' actions were woven into the designs of Providence and guided toward an ultimate good.
- **Fellowship:** The narrative of *The Lord of the Rings* followed the journeys of nine companions brought together for one purpose: the destruction of the One Ring. Through their collective cour-

age, perseverance, and commitment to their quest and each other, they were ultimately victorious.

- **Mercy and pity:** Mercy is central to the story, guiding Tolkien's heroes to act with compassion and empathy. This theme can be seen most prominently in Frodo's relationship with Gollum.
- **Authority and dominion:** Whereas Tolkien's heroes worked in cooperation with the natural order and autonomy of other created beings, Tolkien's villains were willing to manipulate, dominate, and violate the rights of others in pursuit of power. Sauron saw the created world and its inhabitants as tools for his own use; noble characters such as Galadriel, Gandalf, Aragorn, Tom Bombadil, and Treebeard instead respected the dignity, free will, and inherent worth of creation.
- **Mortality:** While dealt with more explicitly in *The Silmarillion*, the theme of mortality still remains prominent in *The Lord of the Rings*. Whereas the lifespan of the elves was tied to the life of the earth, the lives of humans were brief and their fate after death unknown. For both the Nazgûl and Gollum, Sauron's power unnaturally extended their lives, subverting the plans of Ilúvatar.
- **Courage:** Courage drove Tolkien's heroes to accomplish great deeds; *The Lord of the Rings* teaches us that even the smallest hobbits are capable of awe-inspiring courage.
- **Hope against despair:** Hope is presented as the antidote to despair. Tolkien uses examples of the natural world such as the rising sun or the light of the stars to signal a renewal of hope.
- **Pride and humility:** As Frodo's quest reached its conclusion in the heart of Mount Doom, it became clear that Sauron's pride brought about his downfall. By contrast, it was Frodo's humility and complete surrender to his quest that allowed him to get as far as he did.
- **Duty and love:** Characters such as Sam Gamgee are driven by love. A strong sense of duty is emphasized as well, particularly

in the context of war, as seen in the characters of Aragorn and Faramir.

Three Foundational Principles

Tolkien's essay "On Fairy-Stories" is key to understanding his approach to fantasy and myth and how he related his own faith to his work. Written in 1939, this essay was presented by Tolkien as the Andrew Lang Lecture at the University of St. Andrews in Scotland. Andrew Lang was a Scottish poet, novelist, literary critic, and anthropologist with a love for folk and fairy tales. Tolkien's paper began as a response to Lang's work as a folklorist and collector of fairy tales, but it grew into something much more. Often referred to as Tolkien's literary manifesto, "On Fairy-Stories" introduces three major concepts that are essential to laying the groundwork for this book: eucatastrophe, the true myth, and sub-creation.

Eucatastrophe

Tolkien coined the term "eucatastrophe"—the good catastrophe—and defined it as a sudden turn of events that brings about the unexpected happy ending in a story. Eucatastrophe produces a joy that pierces the heart; sorrow is not forgotten or cast away but rather washed over with joy, the two mingled as one.

Eucatastrophe is directly inspired by Tolkien's beliefs in Christianity; it is a concept inextricably linked to the life, death, and Resurrection of Christ. Tolkien explained, "The birth of Christ is the eucatastrophe of man's history. The Resurrection is the eucatastrophe of the story of the Incarnation" ("On Fairy-Stories"). Tolkien considered this unforeseen consolation and happy ending to a narrative to be the highest function of fairy-story. He felt all good stories should mirror what he understood to be the greatest story ever written: the Gospel.

Eucatastrophe builds upon the principle that a higher power (often referred to as Fate) is at work in all things, guiding us toward goodness. Unlike *deus ex machina*, the literary device that amounts to an intervention of the author from outside of the believable plot, eucatastrophe may be surprising, but its logic ultimately derives from the story itself.

The True Myth

Tolkien viewed God as the supreme storyteller, the author of humanity and history. He believed that story was essential to the human relationship with God; because God has written our lives into being, we can respond and participate in his creative power by writing stories of our own. While we exist within the "primary world" of reality, all stories exist within their own "secondary world."

In his poem "Mythopoeia," Tolkien argued that myths were not merely falsehoods or lies, but partial reflections of a supreme myth. Tolkien believed that the Christian myth is not only true in the secondary world, but that it is true in our primary world as well—it is the "true myth." The truth of Christianity, to Tolkien, is at the very root of reality, and all other myths contain elements of it in one way or another.

Sub-creation

The notion of sub-creation is fairly straightforward: Creation is the province of God alone; as the supreme creator, only God can create something from nothing. Sub-creation, as it follows, is the act of creating from other things. Tolkien asserts that "we make still by the law in which we're made" ("Mythopoeia"), calling us sub-creators and connecting the endeavors of our lives to the wider history of the world.

As beings created by God, we emulate him by our own acts of sub-creation. Because God is the supreme author, writing is an act of sub-creation; where God is the supreme artist, making art is an act of sub-creation. Though we have fallen from grace because of sin, we maintain this sense of dignity and purpose as beings created by God, and we speak to that dignity and purpose with our own acts of sub-creation.

Sub-creation is a concept readers will see most clearly illustrated in the pages of *The Silmarillion* when the Vala Aulë created the dwarves in secret. He was confronted by Eru Ilúvatar about the nature of creation, during which Ilúvatar explained to Aulë that he did not have the power to give life to the dwarves: "For thou hast from me as a gift thy own being only, and no more; and therefore the creatures of thy hand and mind can live only by that being, moving when thou thinkest to move them, and if thy thought be elsewhere, standing idle" (*Silm*, ch. 2).

Tolkien underscored in this passage the principle that sub-created beings cannot give life in the same way that God can. Ultimately, Aulë's humility in this moment brought repentance and reconciliation with Ilúvatar; and because Ilúvatar was merciful, the dwarves were given a fullness of life through Ilúvatar himself. Aulë's act of sub-creation was redeemed and folded into Ilúvatar's plan. In a similar way, all of our own sub-creative endeavors can reflect the majesty and ultimate will of God's creation.

Appendix C
Celebrating Tolkien

Three dates in particular hold a special significance for the Tolkien fan community: January 3, March 25, and September 22. There are, of course, others but these are good starting points. All of these days are great opportunities to celebrate the works of Tolkien by spending time with your communities.

Tolkien's Birthday

January 3 is Tolkien's birthday. It is a commonly held tradition among Tolkien fans to gather and make a toast in his honor on the evening of the 3rd of January. The most popular toast is simply, "To the Professor!"

Tolkien Reading Day

March 25 is the date on which the One Ring was destroyed and the realm of Sauron ended. It has since been dubbed Tolkien Reading Day. Since 2003, the Tolkien Society has celebrated March 25 as Tolkien Reading Day by encouraging fans around the world to spend time with their favorite Tolkien passages, to share Middle-earth with those they hold dear, and to host or attend Tolkien-inspired community events online or locally.

This yearly celebration occurs on the 25th of March due to two events that occur in Tolkien's Legendarium: primarily, the downfall of Sauron with the destruction of the One Ring in T.A. 3019; it also coincides with the birth of Elanor the Fair, daughter of Samwise

Gamgee, in T.A. 3021. On this day, we celebrate the passing of the Shadow and the returning of new life to Middle-earth.

Catholics might know March 25 as another day of significance: the Solemnity of the Annunciation, the feast on which we celebrate the coming of the angel Gabriel to invite Mary to bear Jesus as God's Son. As someone whose life was steeped in the liturgical tradition, Tolkien would have been aware of this date's symbolic weight.

Typically, Tolkien Reading Day is celebrated by fans gathering together, whether locally or online, to read their favorite Tolkien passages aloud.

Hobbit Day

September 22 is the birthday of both Frodo and Bilbo Baggins and is often referred to as Hobbit Day. Since our first celebration in 2011, our annual Hobbit Party has easily become one of our favorite annual family traditions. As the years have gone by and our family has grown, our Hobbit Parties have grown with us—what started as an all-day *The Lord of the Rings* movie marathon has eventually become a weekend-long festival filled with food, drink, and games for the whole family. Typically, these celebrations are focused very heavily on food and cheer and song. For recipes, activities, printable resources, and more, please visit teawithtolkien.com/party.

Connecting with Other Tolkien Fans

The Tolkien fandom asks: What if the real Fellowship of the Ring was the friends we made along the way? One of the best things about Tolkien is the way that his stories can bring people together. Whether online or in person, the Tolkien fan community continues to thrive after all of this time. There are so many ways to connect with other Tolkien fans to form genuine friendships and community—all you have to do is take the first step.

Locally and In Person

While it may be daunting at first, connecting with other Tolkien fans in person can be edifying and fun. When looking to find others who are also interested in Tolkien, I recommend joining a local Tolkien society chapter, called a "smial." An updated list can be found on the Tolkien Society website, at www.tolkiensociety.org/society/smials. Each smial has a Facebook group or some other kind of online forum that you can join in order to stay up-to-date on events and discussions. In addition, there are dozens of Tolkien societies and organizations around the world. Tolkien Gateway keeps an updated list at www.tolkiengateway.net/wiki/Tolkien_societies.

Attending Events

Within the Tolkien fan community, conferences or celebrations are often referred to as "moots." Much like an Ent-moot, fans gather to connect, discern, discuss, celebrate, and more. Each of these events has their own distinct purpose and environment, some leaning more academic and others leaning more festive:

- Oxonmoot is the largest of these moots, hosted by the Tolkien Society in Oxford annually each autumn.
- WestMoot is a new annual conference hosted by the Tolkien Society in the United States.
- Signum University hosts several regional moots each year, with their largest being Mythmoot.
- TheOneRing.net maintains a presence at several comic conventions each year, including San Diego Comic-con, New York Comic-con, and Dragon-con across the United States.

I would recommend any of these events as a wonderful opportunity to connect with other Tolkien fans.

Connecting Online

If you enjoyed this book, the Tea with Tolkien online community might be a good fit for you. While the community exists across social media platforms, we primarily gather within our Discord server. To learn more about our Discord server and to join, visit www.teawithtolkien.com/discord. A list of other online community recommendations can also be found at teawithtolkien.com/connect.

Appendix D

Recommended Reading

More of Tolkien's Writing

As briefly mentioned in this book's introduction, there is so much more to Tolkien than *The Lord of the Rings*. Here are a few recommendations for anyone who would like to dive even deeper.

- *The Letters of J. R. R. Tolkien: Revised and Expanded Edition,* edited by Humphrey Carpenter (2023): An invaluable collection of over three hundred of Tolkien's letters sent throughout his lifetime.
- *Unfinished Tales of Númenor and Middle-earth* (1980): A variety of stories and essays left unfinished by Tolkien, edited and published by Christopher Tolkien.
- *The History of Middle-earth* (12-volume set, final volume published 1996): For those interested in learning about how Tolkien's stories developed over the years, these volumes detail the progression and evolution of Tolkien's drafts and notes into their final published versions.
- *The Fall of Númenor,* edited by Brian Sibley (2022): A brilliant compilation of all of Tolkien's writings on the Second Age into one narrative structure.
- *The Nature of Middle-earth,* edited by Carl Hostetter (2021): A compilation of Tolkien's writings regarding the physics and metaphysics of Middle-earth, such as the physical and spiritual attributes of its peoples, animal and plant life, theological and metaphysical themes, and more.

- *Tales from the Perilous Realm* (expanded edition, 2008): A compilation of short stories by Tolkien, including "Roverandom," "Farmer Giles of Ham," "The Adventures of Tom Bombadil," "Leaf by Niggle," "Smith of Wootton Major," and "On Fairy-Stories." These stories are largely disconnected from Tolkien's Legendarium, with the exception of Tom Bombadil's appearance.
- "Mythopoeia" can be read in *Tree and Leaf* (1964).

More about Tolkien's Life

- *J. R. R. Tolkien: A Biography*, by Humphrey Carpenter: The authorized biography of Tolkien.
- *Tolkien and the Great War*, by John Garth: This biography paints an immersive picture of Tolkien's life in the years leading up to, during, and after the First World War.
- *Tolkien's Faith: A Spiritual Biography*, by Holly Ordway: This biography follows Tolkien's life as it was shaped by his Catholic faith.

Middle-earth Resources

- *The Complete Guide to Middle-earth*, by Robert Foster (updated, 2022).
- *The Atlas of Middle-earth*, by Karen Wynn Fonstad (1991).
- *The Silmarillion Reader's Guide*, by Kaitlyn Facista, available for free download at www.teawithtolkien.com/shop.

More about Tolkien's Other Influences

- *Tolkien's Library: An Annotated Checklist*, by Oronzo Cilli (2019): A detailed catalog of the books Tolkien read, consulted, bought, or borrowed.

- *Tolkien's Modern Reading*, by Holly Ordway (2021): While Tolkien was famously a scholar of ancient texts, this book takes a close look at the modern authors who influenced Tolkien.
- *J. R. R. Tolkien. A Secret Vice: Tolkien on Invented Languages*, edited by Dimitra Fimi and Andrew Higgins (2016).
- *Sub-creating Arda: World-building in J. R. R. Tolkien's Works, Its Precursors, and Legacies*, edited by Dimitra Fimi and Thomas Honegger (2019).
- *The Road to Middle-Earth: How J. R. R. Tolkien Created a New Mythology*, by Tom Shippey (2014).

Helpful Tolkien Websites

- **Tolkien Gateway:** www.tolkiengateway.net. The J. R. R. Tolkien encyclopedia built by fans.
- **The Digital Tolkien Project:** digitaltolkien.com. A scholarly project focused on Tolkien from both a corpus linguistic and digital humanities perspective. The "Search Tolkien" feature is an invaluable tool.
- **Tolkien Collector's Guide:** www.tolkienguide.com. An online hub for Tolkien scholarship and news.
- **The Tolkien Society:** www.tolkiensociety.org. All members of the Tolkien Society are granted digital access to the full library of the society's publications, offering insight into decades of Tolkien fandom and scholarship.

Appendix E

PRAYERS RECOMMENDED BY TOLKIEN

After spending the Christmas of 1943 safely at home with his family, Christopher Tolkien returned to his military post amidst the horrors of the Second World War. Tolkien wrote a letter to Christopher to offer words of comfort and advice, urging him to remember his guardian angel, to take every opportunity to receive the Sacraments, and to pray as often as he was able.

In particular, Tolkien recommended making "a habit of the 'praises,'" suggesting several prayers including, "the Gloria Patri, the Gloria in Excelsis, the Laudate Dominum; the Laudate Pueri Dominum (of which I am specially fond), and one of the Sunday psalms; and the Magnificat; and also the Litany of Loretto (with the prayer Sub tuum praesidium). If you have these by heart you never need words of joy."

Listed below are several of these recommended prayers. Because Tolkien himself recommended these prayers in Latin, I have included Latin translations for each as well as English.

The Gloria Patri

English: Glory (be) to the Father, and to the Son, and to the Holy Spirit. As it was in the beginning, is now, and ever shall be, world without end. Amen.

Latin: *Gloria Patri, et Filio, et Spiritui Sancto. Sicut erat in principio, et nunc, et semper, et in saecula saeculorum. Amen.*

The Gloria in Excelsis

English: Glory to God in the highest, and peace on earth to men of good will. We praise you, we bless you, we adore you, we glorify you, we give you thanks for your great glory. Lord God, heavenly King, God the Father Almighty. Lord Jesus Christ, only begotten Son, Lord God, Lamb of God, Son of the Father, who takes away the sins of the world, have mercy on us. Receive our prayer. You sit at the right hand of the Father, have mercy on us. For you alone are the Holy One, you alone are the Lord, you alone are the Most High, Jesus Christ, with the Holy Spirit, in the glory of God the Father. Amen.

Latin: *Gloria in excelsis Deo et in terra pax hominibus bonae voluntatis. Laudamus te, benedicimus te, adoramus te, glorificamus te, gratias agimus tibi propter magnam gloriam tuam, Domine Deus, Rex caelestis, Deus Pater omnipotens. Domine Fili unigenite, Iesu Christe, Domine Deus, Agnus Dei, Filius Patris, qui tollis peccata mundi, miserere nobis; qui tollis peccata mundi, suscipe deprecationem nostram. Qui sedes ad dexteram Patris, miserere nobis. Quoniam tu solus Sanctus, tu solus Dominus, tu solus Altissimus, Iesu Christe, cum Sancto Spiritu in gloria Dei Patris. Amen.*

The Laudate Dominum

English: Praise the Lord, all nations; Praise him, all people. For he has bestowed his mercy upon us, and the truth of the Lord endures forever. Glory be to the Father, and to the Son and to the Holy Ghost; as it was in the beginning, is now, and ever shall be, world without end. Amen.

Latin: *Laudate Dominum, omnes gentes, laudate eum, omnes populi. Quoniam confirmata est super nos misericordia eius et veritas Domini manet in aeternum. Gloria Patri, et Filio, et Spiritui Sancto. Sicut erat in principio, et nunc, et semper, et in saecula saeculorum. Amen.*

Sub Tuum Praesidium

English: We fly to thy patronage, O holy Mother of God; despise not our petitions in our necessities, but deliver us always from all dangers, O glorious and blessed Virgin. Amen.

Latin: *Sub tuum praesidium confugimus, Sancta Dei Genetrix. Nostras deprecationes ne despicias in necessitatibus, sed a periculis cunctis libera nos semper, Virgo gloriosa et benedicta. Amen.*

Prayer for the Beatification of J. R. R. Tolkien

This prayer is intended for private and personal use only:

> O Blessed Trinity, we thank you for having graced the Church with John Ronald Reuel Tolkien and for allowing the poetry of your creation, the mystery of the Passion of your Son, and the symphony of the Holy Spirit, to shine through him and his sub-creative imagination. Trusting fully in your infinite mercy and in the maternal intercession of Mary, he has given us a living image of Jesus the Wisdom of God Incarnate, and has shown us that holiness is the necessary measure of ordinary Christian life and is the way of achieving eternal communion with you. Grant us, by his intercession, and according to your will, the graces we implore [. . .], hoping that he will soon be numbered among your saints. Amen.

Bibliography

Aquinas, Thomas. *Summa Theologica (Complete and Unabridged)*. Translated by Fathers of the English Dominican Province. Coyote Canyon Press, 2018. Kindle.

Birmingham Oratory. "Biography of John Henry Newman." Accessed December 28, 2024. https://birminghamoratory.org.uk/biography.

Carpenter, Humphrey. *J. R. R. Tolkien: A Biography*. Houghton Mifflin, 1977.

Cilli, Oronzo. *Tolkien's Library: An Annotated Checklist*. Luna Press Publishing, 2019.

Drout, Michael D. C., ed. *J. R. R. Tolkien Encyclopedia: Scholarship and Critical Assessment*. Routledge, 2006.

Foster, Robert. *The Complete Guide to Middle-earth*. HarperCollins Publishers, 2022.

Garth, John. *Tolkien and the Great War: The Threshold of Middle-earth*. Houghton Mifflin, 2003.

Hostetter, Carl F. ("Aelfwine"). "A few notes regarding the listing for Tolkien's Copy of Jacques Maritain's *An Introduction to Philosophy*." Tolkien Collector's Guide, May 22, 2024. https://www.tolkienguide.com/modules/newbb/viewtopic.php?postid= 56962#forumpost56962.

Kilby, Clyde S. *Tolkien and The Silmarillion*. Harold Shaw Publishers, 1976.

Kowalska, Maria Faustina. *Diary: Divine Mercy in My Soul*. 3rd ed. Marian Press, 2003.

Newman, John Henry. "The Mission of My Life." Accessed January 31, 2025. https://www.johnhenrynewmancatholiccollege.org.uk/saint-john-henry-newman.

Ordway, Holly. *Tolkien's Faith: A Spiritual Biography*. Word on Fire Academic, 2023.

OSB.org. "The Rule." Accessed January 31, 2025. https://osb.org/our-roots/the-rule.

Rocha, Norma. “Sailing West: Tolkien, the Saint Brendan Story, and the Idea of Paradise in the West.” *Mythlore: A Journal of J. R. R. Tolkien, C. S. Lewis, Charles Williams, and Mythopoeic Literature* 17, no. 4 (1991): 16–20. SWOSU.

Shaw, Roger, ed. *The Book of Saints: A Day-by-Day Illustrated Encyclopedia.* Weldon Owen, 2012.

Thérèse of Lisieux. *Story of a Soul: The Autobiography of St. Thérèse of Lisieux.* Translated by John Clarke, OCD. 3rd ed. ICS Publications, 1997.

Tolkien, J. R. R. *The Hobbit.* Houghton Mifflin, 1937. Kindle.

Tolkien, J. R. R. *The Letters of J. R. R. Tolkien: Revised and Expanded Edition.* Edited by Humphrey Carpenter with Christopher Tolkien. HarperCollins Publishers, 2023.

Tolkien, J. R. R. *The Lord of the Rings* (*Illustrated by the Author*). William Morrow, 2021.

Tolkien, J. R. R. *Morgoth's Ring.* Edited by Christopher Tolkien. Houghton Mifflin, 1993.

Tolkien, J. R. R. *Parma Eldalamberon 17: Words, Phrases and Passages in Various Tongues in The Lord of the Rings.* Edited by Christopher Gilson. Elvish Linguistic Fellowship, 2007.

Tolkien, J. R. R. *Sauron Defeated.* Edited by Christopher Tolkien. Houghton Mifflin, 1992.

Tolkien, J. R. R. *Tree and Leaf.* George Allen & Unwin, 1964.

Tolkien, J. R. R. *Unfinished Tales of Númenor and Middle-earth.* Edited by Christopher Tolkien. Houghton Mifflin, 1980.

Tolkien, J. R. R. *The Silmarillion.* Edited by Christopher Tolkien. Houghton Mifflin, 1977.

KAITLYN FACISTA is the founder of Tea with Tolkien, an online community that celebrates the life, writings, and Catholic faith of J. R. R. Tolkien.

In 2022, she was recognized as a leader in the Tolkien community by the producers of the television series *The Lord of the Rings: The Rings of Power*; in 2024, she was interviewed as a lore expert for an official after-show segment. Facista has spoken on Tolkien's faith, his creative imagination, and the core themes and characters of Middle-earth.

She contributed to a panel at San Diego Comic-Con in 2023 and has been featured in *National Catholic Register* and *Our Sunday Visitor* and on Grotto Network. Her work earned her a spot on the shortlist for the Tolkien Society Awards for "Best Online Content" in 2023 and 2025.

Facista lives with her family in Kokomo, Indiana.

teawithtolkien.com
Facebook: @teawithtolkien
Instagram: @teawithtolkien
Pinterest: @teawithtolkien_
YouTube: @teawithtolkien

THE ROAD GOES EVER EVER ON

Continue on your journey through Tolkien's works with this FREE study guide written by Kaitlyn Facista.

SCAN HERE TO DOWNLOAD